Destorture

By

Rob't Hardin

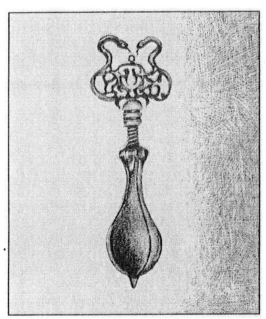

Distorture

by

Rob't Hardin

o

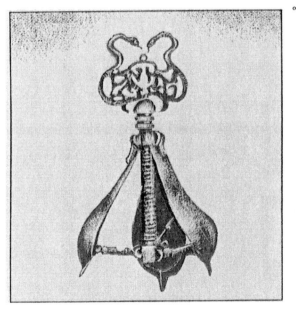

BIB

Normal

Published by FC2 with support given by the English Department
Unit for Contemporary Literature of Illinois State University and
the Illinois Arts Council

Address all inquiries to: FC2, Unit for Contemporary Literature,
Campus Box 4241, Illinois State University, Normal, IL,
61790-4241

Distorture
  Rob Hardin

ISBN: 1-57366-048-5 (paperback)

**Library of Congress Catalog Number
98-071785**

Book Design: Rob Hardin
Cover Design: Todd Michael Bushman

Produced and printed in the United States of America

Acknowledgments:

Some of these stories have been published in slightly different
forms in *Val Demar's Pear*, a chapbook by Permeable Press, and
in *Mississippi Review, Fiction International, Forbidden Acts, Avant
Pop: Fiction for a Daydream Nation, Postmodern Culture, Bomb
Magazine, Red Tape, American Book Review, Black Ice, Airfish,
Sensitive Skin, Nobodaddies, Spitting Image, Proud Flesh, The Cups
Anthology, Future Sex*, and *Funeral Party*.

For Susan Walsh,
and for Elizabeth Mary Brockland,
"Baby-Doll":

*Requiescate in Pace
aut Emergate Quamprimum*

"†**Distorture.** *Obs.* [f. Distort *v.* + -ure; after *torture.*] =
Distorting, Distortion."
—from the *Oxford English Dictionary*

Contents

1	knives for a narcoleptic	11
2	torn from me	25
3	gunpowder come	27
4	still	29
5	hemorrhage	35
6	cadaver-scan	37
7	vein of grace	47
8	dressed to kill yourself	63
9	interrogator frames	77
10	definitions for the dungeon	87
11	i am a monster	95
12	syntax for surgeons	99
13	blood and void	109
14	twenty paradigms	113
15	blowho	115
16	forbidden mammal	117
17	punishment masque	125
18	twenty-five reasons for liking horror	133
19	death is expensive	137
20	technophilia's last wave	141
21	an inquiry into subjective evolution	145
22	when sleep comes down	155

Orchestrations

23	matterland	162
24	di prima: ms. fifty-five	175
25	john quincy adams	185
26	val demar's pear	189

Thanks To:

• Leah Hardin • Larry McCaffery • John Shirley • Perry Meisel •
Sally Cato • Darius James • Julia Solis • Godfrey Diamond •
Colin Raff • Susan Walsh • Nina Meledandri • Nicole Bray •
Claudia Reinhardt • Lynne Tillman • Frederick Nilsen • Jim
Feast • Monica Nelson • Dennis Cooper • Ron Kolm • Jay Jaffe
• Michael Powell • Lou Stathis • Mary Gaitskill • David Ouimet
• Ron Sukenick • Mark Dery • Thom Disch • Robert Coover •
Jeanne Palomino • Curt White • Maggie McDermott • Rhonda
Kitchens • X-Factor • Buddy Meisler • Brian Clark • Debby
Burke • David Dean • Dame Darcy • Anne Archer McDonald •
Michele Amar • Brian Hall • Judy Jackson • Keith Hardin • Eric
Hoffsten • Ian Murdoch • Doug Rice • Jim Goad • Brandon
Wilcox • Jacques Servin • Patrice Haffey • Lauren Sullivan •
Michael Carter •

In Memoriam

Elizabeth Mary Brockland
Susan Walsh
Edward McGranahan
Marky Sliker
Gina Reyna
Mary Miller
Josh Kaufman
Isaac Minsky
Bernard Brounstein

Illustrations

Cover Photo: Claudia Reinhardt
(model: Julia Solis)

Photographs: Anne Arden McDonald

Fig III:	p. 10
Fig IV:	p. 24
Fig V:	p. 38
Fig VI:	p. 154

Drawings: Dame Darcy

| Fig VII: | p. 188 |
| Fig VIII: | p. 205 |

Etchings: David Ouimet

| Fig I: | p. 1, p. 206 |
| Fig II: | p. 3 |

Calligraphy: Michael Powell

| Fig I: | p. 1 |
| Fig II: | p. 3 |

Portrait: Frederick Nilsen

| Fig IX: | p. 208 |

Fig III. *Knives for a Narcoleptic*

Knives For A Narcoleptic

"So I'm touring Europe when we get to Amsterdam," Ratboy is bragging to Schwinn. "It's the middle of summer, drugs all over fuck. I meet this bottled brunette, we both go candyflippin'. I'm fucked up dry-humpin' this girl on a barge and I tell her I wanna have my eyebrow pierced. I can do that, she says. And you don't gotta pay me nothing."

Schwinn listens and nods, waiting for the good part.

"She gets off me, starts feeling around in my bag. You know I'm diabetic, right? Boom. She finds my needles. Starts tryin' to use one on my face. I'm standing there on the barge with this syringe hanging off my eyebrow, blood like drip drip dripping into my eye. I go like this: Forget it. I'm a closet hemophiliac. I dump her. I go to this piercing place. I get it done for seven bucks. The thing I can't take? Is looking at my very own blood."

The moment he feels the light dim, Schwinn stops listening. An August sunset darkens to blood-orange, investing the street with such textures of flesh and decay that even after trying to look bored by it, Schwinn can't deal. Gilded by crimson light, splintered neon signs glimmer like jeweled earwigs. All that's missing is a Hans Bellmer pin-up dipped in grit and chrome, an Ouroboros exhaust pipe in her mouth.

He'd love to stay for the view but break-time is over. It's later than Schwinn, a precocious degenerate on NA training wheels, wants to hang without working on his four-track. Output is key, Schwinn keeps telling Ratboy and Ditch. All day, Rat sidesteps talk of music and the future, changing the subject to The Ritual: Germans tied to trees in the Tenderloin District, strippers gone wet-eyed during the sacrament of blood-book printing. Singers whose stomachs quake under criss-crossed dripping red arcs, modifying the cutter's strokes with shrieks. By the time Schwinn remembers the real subject, Rat is half-way down the street on some cryptic errand—metal case in hand and leaning against the wind like a broom-riding herald.

At the merest mention of The Ritual, Schwinn stares into space. Spent little girls have appealed to him since the age of six. Which is not surprising, since Schwinn's just turned seventeen.

Rat walks over to the entrance of a tenement, looks inside, squints and nods. Must know someone in there, Schwinn figures.

Rat calls for Ditch, whose ass rests on the entrance paneling. A nineteen-year-old with an acne-ravaged face, Ditch snickers as he skitters over like Nosferatu. Snot dries on the vinyl tank-top that sags against his concave stomach and toy-flimsy ribs. He skips a rock with the square point of his wingtip, cocky in designer scruff.

Rat taps his heel in time. Schwinn, he hisses, tattooed neck pinched by the collar of his sand-yellow rayon suit. He points to the hallway, then to the spot next to him. Meaning, get the fuck over here. Schwinn nods and blinks. Still wincing at the nickname he used to like.

Schwinn walks over slowly. The nickname sounded great when Rat christened him in front of some beautiful toss-up.

They all cluster around the girl. Schwinn turns to look, but can't believe what's there: The Ritual in the flesh.

Rat glances at Schwinn. "Quit shaking," he says.

They find her dreaming in the stairwell of an emptied tenement: A woman, aged somewhere between twenty-eight and thirty, with braided black hair and grayish skin. Her slender body is striated with muscle, her limbs splayed and sunken into the curved accordion-fall of stairs. Her skin is misted with soot, her torso segmented and bent like the neck of an exhausted jack-in-the-box.

Dressed for a trip to the store, the girl wears no make-up. Her sheer black top is knotted at the waist. Shreds from short-short cut-offs trail her ass like spittle-strands.

They carry her into the hallway to inspect her abrasions. She is spectacularly scarred: detours to death cross and crease her arms, delimit her limbs. She is bruised with using, cosmetically pierced, hermetically scarified with holes bought and proffered, elaborately scored with the incisions of pins and syringes. Her arteries are as torn as northern highways. She half-awakens and lingers at the threshold: Eyes fluttering, body tremulous with tentative connections.

Rat sets down his teal-blue case. It is metal with a black plastic handle and clip-lock, the kind ordinarily used for carpenter's tools. Inside are four levels of pull-out plastic trays, where Rat carries objects too quirky to categorize without a glossary of trauma: The inside of an ocarina, connected by a copper wire to a speaker ripped from an answering machine. A slim digital card, capable of recording forty seconds of sound, used mostly to play back the squeals of Rat's tabby cat, Bleep. A twist of blonde hair, dipped in something unpleasant to the touch.

On the second tier of the carpenter's tray, clinical metal glints at Schwinn, the kind used in Rat's stories of Ritual. Neither kid has ever seen the last two shelves. About their contents, Ditch has his theories. Schwinn prefers not to guess.

"Stuff in here will come in handy," Rat says.

"Good," Ditch says. Schwinn nods wearily, not wanting to know.

"This is the only way to wake her," Rat says. For the first time Schwinn can remember, Rat opens his case in full view, showing its contents like any Las Vegas magician. He reaches under the first tray and pulls out something serrated. The thing looks like a dental pick, only it has a little wheel on the end with triangular spikes.

"Cool," Ditch says.

"What is it?" Schwinn asks.

"Wurtenburg Pinwheel," Rat says. Holding it out for everyone to see.

"How do you use it?" Schwinn asks. Dazed, he counts the spikes.

"Open your hand," Rat says. Schwinn does as he's told. Twenty-two spikes in all.

Rat drags the wheel across Schwinn's hand. Knife-lightning slices his lifeline, swift and vicious.

"Ahhh!" Schwinn screams, pulling back his hand. "You fuckin' cut me!"

Rat's brows arch over ranging eyes. "Schwinn, Schwinn. Look at your hand. Look. At. Your. Hand."

Schwinn looks at it, amazed: No blood.

"Didn't cut the skin, right? That's 'cause it's not supposed to cut skin. Doctors use it to test people's nerves." Schwinn shakes his head. What he feels is not what he sees.

"Think you can calm down now, you little *shit?*" Rat shouts dramatically.

"I am calm," Schwinn replies, smiling in spite of himself. "I just don't think you should use the spiky thing on her." Behind him, Ditch snorts.

"We have to," Rat says, alive to the white skin below him. "It's the only way to wake her. Trust me: She won't mind."

Rat lifts the girl's semi-sheer top, leaving her black bra in place. Deliberately, he drags the wheel across her cleavage.

14

No marks, not even welts, score her poison-pale skin. But to Schwinn, just watching it happen feels like a rupture. He winces with each narcoleptic twitch.

Rat drags and re-drags the spiky wheel over the girl's stomach, looking for synapse light beneath the skin. But no light rises.

Eyes greed-thin, Ditch clacks his teeth, rakes wall plaster with his nails. If he ever developed the guts, he might disembowel her.

"That didn't work," Rat says, shaking his head. "Guess she's getting tougher."

She probably wouldn't mind being drawn and quartered by Harley Davidson Police Specials. Schwinn can't help respecting that.

Through a round soot-streaked stairwell window, and distantly through swirling squatdust, pink light darkens. The sunset fades like Schwinn's survival instinct. As if his emotion made the darkness grow.

Rat smirks at him. "You like her, right? Don't worry. She'll feel like fucking you when we get her awake."

"Why you look so tired?" Ditch asks Schwinn. Rat rolls his eyes.

Rat turns the girl over on her stomach. He bends her forward and gently pushes back a palmful of black hair as if smoothing a horse's mane. A sudden V crests at the nape of her neck, a widow's peak in reverse. Rat reaches into his case, drags his fist out of the second tier. His hand opens: 28-gauge antique syringes, filigreed with Sarah Bernhard tresses in beveled glass. He holds her throat with one hand. With the other, he carefully pushes the needlepoints into her neck, arranging the syringes in a slack crescent. One by one, he draws 10cc of blood from each. In response, the girl's body begins to tremble. Her eyes do not open, though REM movement hints they might at any time.

She trembles so violently that Rat has to steady the last few syringes. He draws blood from her body as though metering the amount she can lose this round. He empties one of the syringes into his mouth, pulls her head up by the hair and squirts another syringeful between her lips. He offers another syringe to Ditch, who drinks it up eagerly. On some level, Schwinn wants a taste, perhaps even more than the others. But since she's asleep, the sight makes him physically ill. He's not comfortable with the idea of vampire rape.

Rat opens his zipper, squirts a little blood onto his cock. It stiffens. He holds the girl by her hair and masturbates until his erection twitches on automatic. Ditch is instantly in front of the girl, ready to rub himself on her face. "Not yet," Rat says. Schwinn squeezes his tip through his jeans. Yeah, he's hard, but his ribs feel hollow. His stomach's a falling elevator. If he touched her now, he'd tremble, his lids would flutter.

Rat places his thumbs in the hollows of her collarbone, pushes hard. Looks at her eyes, shakes his head. "What do I have to do?"

He unknots her top, takes a grease pencil out of his pocket and draws an elaborate spiral, a biologist's emblem of progenitive dead matter. It's the logo that Rat's latest band, Worship Curve, likes to tattoo on the skins of kick drums. "This is a drawing? Of the neurofibrillary tangle you get in a bad case of Alzheimers," Rat says. He reaches into the case, takes out a little piece of cotton and a bottle of rubbing alcohol. He dips the cotton in the bottle and swabs down the girl's back. Then he takes out a scalpel, dips it in the alcohol like a joint. "The only way to wake her," he chants.

Rat's generation grew up believing that sex = death. No wonder he gets hard whenever he risks disease: For him, the equation works in either direction.

Lovingly, Rat lights a match under the scalpel, sinks the tip through skin and traces pencil lines. He follows the pattern carefully, surrounding it with concentric circles. Schwinn notices that the blood-inked cuts look barbed and tribal, then realizes that's the point. Human beings were doubtless the first books ever made.

In the window, the skylight dims. Ditch chisels schoolboy runes in plaster with a pocket-knife, pretending he's opening the troughs of the narcoleptic's spine. She's like some burial ground to him, some site so charged that the only way to deal is to worship or expose its innards.

"Gimme your sleeve," Rat says. Schwinn's arm goes rigid. He tries not to frown, but the muscles won't unclench.

"C'mon, *c'mon*," Rat says. "This jacket is a piece of shit."

Rat pulls Schwinn over by his sleeve. He soaks up the excess blood with Schwinn's ragged denim jacket. To mark Schwinn with the crime, is that it? Schwinn wants to scream, but he's driven to suffer and stare. A comatose girl is opening him. His ribs feel pithed as if by Ratboy's scalpel.

Rat pulls off his own rayon jacket and turns it inside out. The white lining is a crisscross of primitive patterns in dried blood. Rat finds an empty spot, presses the girl's wounds against the fabric to make an imprint, then flattens the jacket on some papers to let it dry. "Wish I had a paper suit sometimes," he says.

"Me too," Ditch says. Making imprints all over his jeans until Rat says to knock it off.

Schwinn can't understand why doesn't she wake up. "Know what she's dreaming about?" he asks.

"She told me once," Rat answers, looking down at the tips of his winklepickers. "She dreams about being ripped apart by monsters. That's why it's good what we're doing. You think I'm cutting into her, right? But I'm saving her from the one who's really cutting her up."

Or using her because she's helpless, Schwinn says to himself.

Ditch thinks it's funny. "Let's drag her inside some apartment and fuckin' take turns."

But Rat says nothing, and Schwinn just closes his eyes.

Ratboy opens the carpenter's case and slides out three giant needles: As thin as antennae, as long as robot erections.

17

"One for each of us," Rat says, handing a needle to Schwinn. "You'd better go first."

Schwinn holds it, queasy at the thought of plunging it in. "If I'm gonna fuck her, I don't need a prosthetic dick," he says in a faux-manly voice—a voice made even more fake by a sob at the end.

"You don't believe we're s'posed to be doing this," Rat says. Schwinn gasps at his accuracy. "But like I said: I know her. I do this all the time. And right now? We need to try something else."

Rat slips his own needle under the epidermis of her left cheek and pushes it in. She stirs slightly as he holds open her mouth, forcing the needle through until it pierces her left inner cheek. The pin slides through her mouth-space and right inner cheek. There is no blood.

Her mouth swings open. Schwinn imagines a hinge in a party doll's jaw. As if unconsciousness hadn't dehumanized her enough.

When the point emerges from her right cheek, Schwinn recoils—skin stinging as he cringes in her place. Rat pierces one of the girl's temples with the second pin. He starts to hand the last pin to Schwinn but catches himself. Then he withdraws the rest of the pins. He slides them all through a cloth dipped in alcohol and puts them away.

No pain Rat attempts to inflict disturbs the girl. Sensation drives her deeper into sleep, which makes her look saintly. Schwinn would like to marry her for suffering this. He steps closer to her and clutches her hand. He wonders what the fuck she's dreaming about. As surely as insomniac Schwinn flees from sleep, her body remains too tactile, an exhibition. If Rat's correct, she dreams of being peeled.

Schwinn tries to imagine what's in her skull: Whitelight fog pours from a hole in the ceiling. He whispers to her. She murmurs but does not wake. Fleeing her insides, a gallery of ghouls. Fleeing the sadists outside, her gallery's reflection.

He slams down her arm. She stirs slightly, fluttering her lids. Eyes open: When she focuses on him, she looks alarmed. Ashamed, he glances at Rat, who stares back, incredulous.

Then she falls back asleep. Rat sighs.

"Why isn't anything working," he says, grimacing. Recklessly, he douses her shoulders with alcohol. From the bottom of the case, he takes out a barber's straight razor. The blade swings open with a click. The handle reminds Schwinn of a remote control for suffering—something that fits in your hand, grip-ridged and facelessly efficient. Rat offers no verbal picture of his mind or blade. He aims for her shoulders and slashes almost at random.

"Hey, *no,*" Schwinn says. The others draw back, shocked. He stares at the slashes. Their complexity mirrors his idea of perfection.

"What the fuck's wrong with you," Rat says. "I didn't—she ain't hurt. They're hamburger cuts, professionals call them that. Those'll heal right off. As a matter of fact, here, Ditch, why don't you see if you can get her to wake up?" Rat offers Ditch the razor. Ditch grins. Gratefully, his hand slides away from the wall.

That's it. Enough.

Before Ditch can get one step closer to Rat, Schwinn blocks him. "Do *not* give that asshole the razor. I've fucking had enough of this, okay?"

"Brave wuss to step in front of a blade," Ditch says. But stopping Rat takes play, not courage.

Rat looks up at him. "You're fucked. I thought you were into this."

"I don't wanna do this," Schwinn says. "And you know what? Just call me Tim, okay? I'm not a fucking bicycle. Tim says you're gonna fucking stop right now."

Rat sighs, looking drunk and disgusted. "Okay, 'Tim.' Since you just don't seem to get it, I'll stop like you said." Ditch slams the wall. "But I told you: she likes it."

"She's not awake to tell me that," Tim says.

19

Rat looks at the girl. Looks at the case. Looks at the girl, then at Tim. Picks his yellow jacket off the floor and slings it on his shoulder. "Okay," he says. Inside, Tim says *thank you.*

"What the fuck," Ditch says. "My dick is hard."

"By the time we get outside," Rat says ruefully, "it probably won't be."

The three of them drag her out of the hallway, a smashed cardboard box pitched beneath her like a sled. They slide her into the shadows so no one will trample her. Rat arranges her hair around her face, brushing away strands. Tim removes his jacket and spreads it over her. "Check your pockets," Rat says.

"Thanks," Tim says. Paranoiac-thorough, he still finds nothing. He covers her slowly with his jacket, memorizing her face.

Rat shrugs. "I'd put mine over her except for the stains."

Tim closes his eyes, nods. Remembering her.

"Ditch and I are goin' to a Russian bar for a while. Seventh and First. Wanna come?"

"Not really," Tim says. "But thanks all the same."

As they step out of the building, the night sky clarifies Tim's focus, pares his thought to twilight and glittering detail. He thinks maybe he'll wait until the others leave, go back to the tenement and carry her to her house. But where does she live?

"What are you waiting for, Ditch?" Rat says.

They wave each other on. Rat and Ditch meander off to play some pool and possibly get laid. Tim stands there lingering.

When Rat and Ditch get far enough down the street, their personalities lose all gravitational hold on Tim. Compelled, he slips into the space between two ruined buildings. Palms pressed against temples, he's crying for some stupid reason. He knows he'll go home and lie awake worrying about this woman until the sun rises and he tries to follow, feeling totally frail as he mourns without remorse. But before he can writhe in misery and bliss, there's something he has to do.

He thinks about calling a cop. But what if she liked it? What if Rat's telling the truth?

Yeah, right. Doesn't matter what she likes when she's awake. The point is, she wasn't at home to say yes or no.

He drifts back into the tenement, idling again. He can feel the dead slam against the walls and ceiling, jumping up and down in pseudo-fun. Meringue and Selina blast through apartment doors.

He goes to the Korean place on the corner, buys rubbing alcohol and a little wheel of gauze. The old grocer looks at him quizzically, expression etched with a question that doesn't care. Tim goes back to the hallway. He slides the girl out of the shadows. He swabs her down with the gauze and alcohol, lingering on the cuts. For the first time, he notices the skin on her chest is scalloped. He touches it: soft and wrinkly. Scar tissue makes babies of us all. He's probably only ever lost it about girls with scars.

He swabs the blood off her stomach, the edges of the scalpel's lineations still transparent white. He puts his lips to the design, feels horrible, pulls away. Then sneaks another look, lives there for days.

He ministers to her back, imagining scenarios in which he alone cares for her—his whispered enchantments resurrecting her health. Above them, someone bangs on pipes. He freezes, catches sight of a tiny retreating gray tail: relax, it's a rat. He tends to her neck, lifts her arms, slips her tremulous hands through jacket-sleeves. Then buttons everything, including the collar. Lays gauze-strips over that, a mummy's blanket.

He takes out his pen and scratches down his number. Starts to put it in the jacket pocket: too obvious. Finds her change purse, shoves in the paper, bent and semi-legible. If she finds it, she probably won't call. Dumb idea, he says to himself.

Carefully, he slips the purse strap around her waist. My job here is done, he telegraphs to an imaginary inspector. He exits the building and studies the cracks in the street. When he thinks about leaving, an invisible finger snags his collar. More real than ones he just touched, it knows what it wants.

Swearing, he picks up the pay phone and calls the cops. An unintelligible voice obscures a pre-written salutation: Police, Operator Nine-Two-One-Five, where is the emergency?

"I'd like to report an unconscious girl in a hallway."

Can you describe her?

"She's around twenty-six, maybe Jewish, braided black hair. Skinny, cut up bad. Wearing denim cut-offs and a tied top. Beautiful, except for the cuts."

When you say cut up, sir, would you describe her as being in need of medical attention?

"Not really. No."

Where is she located?

"113 E. 6th St."

Thank you. An officer will be there as soon as possible. Would you like to leave your name?

"Not really. Not this time." Click.

He returns to the spot where he and Ratboy "met" her. Stands looking at her from the recessed doorway, face crescented in shadow. Projecting his stupid longing onto her skin, a blank marquee. Walks over and kisses her one last time: this is it. How weird to think she'll wake and never know him.

A blank marquee? Well, no. That's not it exactly. What her slashed skin really means to him is something vague. It's more like a watchtower lamp he'll try to picture until the strain starts a ravenous flash-fire of guilt. He'll elevate its flame to angel status, condemning himself to watching her pain replay. He'll keep looping the whole event in his head, her tenement. In some versions, he'll stop the others from cutting her. In others, she'll wake, they'll instantly fall in love. In versions barely admitted, he lovingly cuts her. Until all versions blur into shots of his mother crying.

A few cars pass. Horn-blasts bending and dwindling, held notes from Gloomy Sunday's morphine trombones. Tim shakes himself.

A man in a wheelchair watches: sunglasses and shorts, stumps dangling over the seat.

In the distance, that clarion siren. Tim backs out of the doorway staring. Night night, he whispers. Night night. He leaves her there sleeping.

Fig IV. *Torn From Me*

Torn From Me

SHE WAS A SUGARPALE STREETCORNER WHORE with eyes like cracked blue marbles and a smile frosted as white as windshield mist. Through afternoon traffic, she gazed at me like a dream of a passing chance, but she never stopped hustling no matter how wasted she became. At dusk, anticipation kept me awake until she huddled against my threshold, shivering in fishnets. When the buzzer summoned, I raced to that drop-stop on the steps of desolation.

Without realizing it, I soon fell straight to hell—waiting and praying whenever she showed up late. One day, she stopped coming. After a week, the loss itched like an anthive pitched between my ribs.

I trawled the alleys looking for her, quizzing pimps who worked on stupefied stares whenever I mentioned her name. Slowly, I traced the fame and shame her voice cast like a visor-blue shadow. The starker my sample of Lydia's streetwalker past, the graver my taste for a love I couldn't shake. So I slept in her depths, awakened in her wake, lived on the slivers of facts long ago retained.

Finally, I was alone in that attic, reconstructing her loss like a surgeon of recollection. I couldn't understand why I was compelled to do it—why she drew me to that place where decay slips into *nothing*. I wanted to forget but amnesia never erased the flavor. I could only relive those polluted nights *in memoriam;* could only commemorate the times I last saw her alive; where passion swam, submerged in the past—which is, of course, the only thing that lasts.

Gunpowder Come

He spotted her on the Fourth of July in a place misted with the smoke of cherry bombs. Krane was standing in the doorway of Embargo Books, listening to "Do It Like A G. O." by the Geto Boys. Rap lyrics and the smell of gunpowder made Norfolk Street feel like a site of terrorist resistance. But slogans of defiance turned alchemical when a figure emerged from the tinted fumes.

She came into view slowly, turning the corner as the yellow haze began to clear. Something was wrong with her face—it was a tragi-comic mask of slackness and rigidity. But beneath this oxymoronic expression lay the cast of a Botticelli angel: Roman nose, flared nostrils, wide, dark eyes like those of a cat in shadow. She was quite beautiful, even though she had been tortured to the point of temporary paralysis.

A bracelet of string dipped in blood and cerebrospinal fluid hung knotted around her wrist. Intricate with tangles, its drippings were medieval and complex, a lithographed waterfall of crosses and scythes. Had this decoction of tears been drawn from her body or her lover's? Both had been imprisoned under the guise of drug auditing, but only one had emerged to meet him. Was she being released out of mercy, or to warn him of the consequences of rebellion?

As she approached, the temperature of his body changed in sympathy. He touched her fist and shivered when it opened. His nerves accessed her sense-memory, compelling teletacit voices to *shriek* more information than interrogators could hope to extract.

She had been broken into like a box of murder. After twisting her head apart in search of explosives, suppression probes had found only semantic fragments— secrets in a language so evanescent that it passed for air. But Krane knew why she was crypted inside. His nerves reached through the veneer of transparence, probing like antennae for the bloody country behind the wall.

Chained to the corpses of her own family for weeks, she had learned to associate the proximity of love with the maggots of decomposition. Interrogators had starved her until she was forced to reify the faces of her loved ones—first with revulsion, then with hunger. In the official report, clerks had suggested that her paralysis was the result of a disease caused by cannibalism, but this was unlikely. Precipitated by famine, exhaustion and dehydration, the climax of her stroke was physical collapse.

Scenes of death had become sites of orgasm. Her legs nearly buckled as she tipped her pelvis toward Krane, chilling his synapses with spurts of information. Seconds of pleasure swelled into pictures which obliterated the reality of Norfolk Street: her legless mother, opened at the waist. The castrated cadaver of her father, cheekbones blunted by sandpaper. And at the center of a prison floor, an excrescence of tissue and pliant marrow: the remains of her four-month-old son. The interrogators had opened his screaming smile with knives; it was only at the moment of release that she could endure his rape. Tortured by the absence of torture, her come was dust. A sandpainting of empty bodies and fixed lamprey eyes.

Still

He wasn't drunk or paralytic, and no one had put him under hypnosis. The X-K seemed to have fooled around with some dangerous strain of boredom, then wandered into a trance through a door that locked automatically. Motionless from his tensed shoulders to his gangly legs, he was the image of an ollie hanging out. Some photo-realist might have sculpted his look of lobotomized bliss.

Like the windshields of showroom cars, his eyes merely framed the absence of the owner. They were wading-pool blue and glimmered above his small, sunburnt nose. His lips were thick, chapped, the color of scarlet model paint. Long ash-blond curls fell to the ridged neck, just touching the over-developed deltoids. The chest and groin were striped with shadow under half-drawn venetian blinds.

The white room was big, empty. It contained only black furniture. The blinds, metal chair and cubed coffee table gleamed with streaks of sunlight. The black-sheeted mattress reflected nothing. Stage center, it drooped over a board mounted on some concrete blocks. The X-K sat on the mattress. He was still except for his legs, which rocked slightly as they dangled over the bedboard.

The man who lived there slanted against the doorpost, his frame a limp diagonal. He couldn't understand how the kid had gotten past two dead-bolt locks and a steel door—

a tall order, especially for someone whose mind was missing. Fortyish, slight, the man pushed sharpened fingernails through silver-black hair. His eyes curved to inverted U's as he sized up the X-K's oblivious body.

In the hallway, mounted on vinyl-coated steel rods: a compact disc player, turntable and cassette machine. In the bedroom, discreetly wired above the windows: thin white speakers. Mahler's *Kindertotenlieder* poured from them, filling the room with its *fin de siècle* necrophrenia. Next to the amplifier, various records and tapes: SPK, Gesualdo, *Deploration On The Death Of Ockeghem*.

The man walked to the window, drew the blinds, then moved to the closet. Parting the rack in the middle, he pulled out lace-up leather pants and a shirt of cherry-red silk. He slid into them, then slipped into black boots of soft Italian leather. Last of all, he chose a black medieval waistcoat. He ran two fingers along its raised pattern of scythes, stopped at the breast pocket, and reached in.

He dragged out a cigarette and held a match to it, staring at the X-K the whole time. Like storerooms that once contained important negatives, the eyes led to an absence. The X-K's *Body* seemed a better canvas than the eyes: its musculature had been eccentrically developed. So much wreckage lay under the surface that it was as if a breastplate of spears threatened to rise through the Body's skin.

The man studied the Body for a few seconds, approached it, and dropped to a kneeling position.

Tilted between thumb and forefinger, butt of the filter pushed forward by the thumb, the cigarette drew zigzags of smoke across the chest. The (visual) process implied deeper operations: the cigarette was *evocative*, a light pencil tracing wave-forms on the screen of a Synclavier. Afternoon chilled to evening; as if in response to the cigarette's floating graphics, the Body began to shudder.

The man pointed his cigarette at the xiphoid process. He considered burning a mark there, then dismissed the idea.

There was no reason to disfigure the Body with a grid that would rise in welts. The thought of inflicting pain left him indifferent: any damage to the skin would prove too literal for the imagination to distort. The Synclavier screen would freeze under the Medusa-gaze of Violence, and discoloration would be the only added dimension in place of numerous subtractions.

The jagged lines began to straighten and intersect. A moment of extreme pleasure took him over as the grid of smoke tightened against The Body. The tautening lines resembled laces that were slowly being pulled through a series of obliquely-positioned holes. He blew smoke rings against this—one for the hollow of each violin-soundboard hip—and the rings complicated the lattice-work to Art Nouveau.

As the window's square of sky dimmed, the glow of the cigarette ash grew brighter: it became an arrowhead of raw meat under the violet lamp of a science exhibit. Trembling slightly, the Body paled to black-light-poster garish as bands of smoke rose to restrain the shoulders. At last, it was encased in a suit of ghostly white bondage gear.

The Body shuddered in the draft. Bumps rose in patches on its chest and stomach, streaks reddened across the white shoulders. Tiny slash-marks appeared where the sleeping skin smarted most under the fumes.

Lesions formed between the costal margin and the linea sublunaris. The lesions widened and spread below the xiphoid process; they spat threads of black smoke which climbed the thorax, deserted the Body at the upper deltoids, and gathered into blurred bars. The bars crumbled into black dots which formed shadowy, Seraut-like representations of nucleated cells. The cells were bound into spirochetes, and these gathered into whorls. The smoke had become a pointillist's animated cartoon of the morphology of multi-cellular animals.

The skin surrounding the nipples cracked and healed

31

repeatedly, as in a case of fast-motion eczema. The area soon resembled a cartographer's map of layered transparencies.

The sunset was of epic duration. Lingering streaks dangled in the mirror like an homage to Calder. In contrast, the Body's scars healed in the tangerine light as in a fast-motion film, until the cartography of lesions and ruptured tissue smoothed to uninflected white.

The man exhaled sharply. He could not account for the series of Herschel Gordon Lewis mutilations he had just performed. He calmed himself, lit another cigarette, and returned to the Body.

As before, the chest writhed under blurred restraints. Roman X's bound the torso, and a mesh of fine ash tightened around the tremulous frame.

Particles of red smoke seemed to magnetize lit cigarettes *inside* the Body: red tips pressed through its smoking skin.

The space between the ribs and stomach, and another directly below the navel, filled with pus until they began to swell and pulsate. Bumps appeared on these areas; the bumps darkened, blistered, opened. The muscles and tissue below these began to bulge. The upper chest and navel were invisibly pulled in opposite directions until the waist and ribs were twisted open.

Pieces of the Body began to fly around the room.

The man trembled with release. Fissures opened in his chest, spuming with ejaculate until he was completely drained. His lids closed slowly, like power windows. Through them, he saw the yellow of oncoming headlights. The yellow intensified to white until, when sleep came down, even that empty color had been erased.

As the *Kindertotenlieder* ended, the two Bodies slumped to the floor.

Integuments lifted themselves slightly from the lacerations and veins wriggled out. These flew to the center of the room, knotted themselves into an arabesque, and hardened into a green partition, which stood between the Bodies.

The partition was divided into two halves. Its design revealed droll figurations which, seen at a distance of a few yards, proved to depict an unusually violent masque.

The organs featured in the masque were impaled on an arabesque that, in the style of Art Nouveau at its most excessive, represented a kind of serrated circuitry.

At the center of the arabesque, trefoil components outlined the disfigured body of Origen. Two keyholes formed the stylized wound in his side. Drops of blood hung in a chain from each keyhole, and each chain extended laterally to an antipodally positioned object. The right chain led to a burning trilobite, the left, to a brain sealed in fire. The pointed flames which surrounded each object terminated in a band of smoke that curved diagonally to the top of the arabesque. There, both bands joined in an ogee and, at its vertex, spelled the word *PASSIVITY* in skywritten characters.

The room dimmed.

The delicate lineations of the arabesque drooped, then tore, until the partition came apart in ragged halves.

The two veinless Bodies flattened like deflating beach toys, molding themselves to the wood-grain of the floor. Only the man's head remained erect. It swelled to hydrocephalic, and its lips began to move.

Invisibly, a phonograph stylus clicked against a record label. Forced by the record's spiral groove, it endlessly repeated this action at the interval of a double-dotted quarter note.

The man's mouth twitched in time with the clicking stylus. The ticcing was violent, parodistic, and was soon accompanied by a periodic bulging of the eyes.

A string section see-sawing between two unrelated chords—C major and E-flat minor—and bassoons and tympani answering each other with absurd trills, grew faintly audible between clicks.

33

As the light continued to dim, only the twitching head moved. Even the monotony of its ticcing suggested a kind of stasis.

The room went black, but the noise persisted like an after-image.

Hemorrhage

In relationships, I am John Wayne Gacy, in self-deception, Oliver North. Your indifference is our hinge. When I look at you, I see lips fixed with duct tape. Your body wrapped in telephone wire. The ironies of bondage underscore the objectivity of your gaze. Our eyes form symmetries, like the black seeds in a halved apple. We live for the suffering of the gifted.

My hatred streams from a past so glacial I can't feel the radix. My memory is like my body: frostbitten. But when I take apart some human toy, the humiliation comes back in flashes. As he dies, fistfuls of glitter are thrown in my face. I like how the eyes freeze—the pupils transfixed like test patterns. It makes me aware of the bones in my hands.

But seconds of recognition are followed by decades of ice. So when I write to the papers, I replace the buried world with explanations. *Burned by the stove, I became a pyro. My ego wanted Daddy, so my id set fire to dogs.*

Lucky for you you're not a boy. We met on an off-ramp to Victoria. I was fleeing a nation of corpses, you were looking for new ways to pulverize your cervix. We both liked fear, but there wasn't any friction between us. We were too comfortable with our taste for pain.

We wanted a three-way and the privileged had no right to live. So we decided to go shopping. It was easy to park by the private school, to pretend to be your chauffeur. To find a miniature Midas and a motel to keep him in. The kid made it easy by sending out a distress signal. It issued from the ice age of his infancy. He'd had his own glaciers to thaw.

We talk like shrinks, but we fuck like born killers. That's why a gasping child splits you open. At an age when most children feel immortal, this one is begging for death. Asking for the black train out of suburbia. Away from the white-haired couples, with their tiny dogs and dying lawns. But before oblivion stops his eyes, he must be shown the rebus of his own entrails. Like Gumby-blobs in a claymation cartoon, his guts arrange themselves into scenes:

In the Criminal Saints' Memorial Chapel, Van Gogh stands on his head, his pate resting on a throne of electrodes. Neurologists feed him handfuls of Dilantin. Through the window, he connects with the stars—gleaming perforations in black bone. Curtains flail the vent. Electrical storms within the brain overlay his vision. His lids are a cosmology of exploding glass.

The chapel fills with eyeless women, their cheeks dripping, their sockets glowing like orange wallets. Van Gogh is still upside down, but the neurologists have nailed him to a dollar sign. The legend I. N. D.—*short for* Indifference, Neutered Dog—*is scored above his legs. "Money burns," he shouts. The women touch the inverted emblem with charred fingers.*

The church explodes. Trapped in the pocket of the explosion, a flock of blue-jays dissolves. Their bone-dust floats like a powder parasol. It drifts over an L. A. club called Slandergraph. Outside, a spent designer vomits her own intestines, curlicues of leather and velour. They circle the blast like whips of shame. Her fluids condense to a miniature storm cloud. It floats over a nearby suburb, drenching a park with spittle. Her scalp floats in the swimming pool, a cauldron of amber water.

What brilliant sparks leap from the genes of the disinherited. As with his entrails, so with his eyes. But before he passes out, the boy must be given an explanation: nothing personal, kid. Even though there was rape along the way.

Listen, asshole, it isn't a matter of conscience. Soldiers of misfortune don't give a shit about casualties. The class that dismissed me taught the world to believe in breeding. So we've come to this reunion dressed as executioners. To harvest the pedigreed in their prime.

It's too bad you've more to live for than wretches like us. I used to watch your car ascend the hill as I hid in the briars. I'd picture your face behind mirrored glass, as safely ensconced as a trust fund. I'd conjure you in my book-crazed daydreams, willing you to lick the dirt off my fingers because I thought we should trade places. Back then, I wanted to be you. Now I content myself with wearing your rich boy skin.

This isn't the first time an outcast's headline was a prince's obituary. My name has swallowed yours like a python—swelling with its prominence, feeding on its prestige. You're the end of the line, the insipid bearer of a bankrupt title. But I am the gourmet of nightmare. Excreted through me to a public of losers, passed down to your inferiors on bloodied china, your fragments are your fate. A last call to public service. Bred for privilege, bread for slaughter.

Fig V. *Cadaver-Scan*

Cadaver-Scan

Leave them only their eyes to weep with.
— Prince Otto Eduard Leopold von Bismarck,
1st Chancellor of the German Empire,
directing his men in the war of 1870

<u>MAY 21, 1992</u>. Just looking down at the pavement from his third-story loft made Giz feel claustrophobic. The view was needle-shaft narrow: curbs congested with double-parked bridge and tunnel trade, a chalked-off basketball game blocking East Fourth Street. The horizon wasn't much better. At vision's limit, he discerned a phalanx of tenements that swayed like sick bums leaning. Above it, the sky looked so polluted that the noon glare offered no more light than smudged neon. But the stratosphere's gun-metal gray felt deeper than the screen he saw when he tried to rest his eyes.

Through a diamond-shaped space in the window gate, he squinted at the walkway between Avenues C and D. A gritty lot the color of sprayed roaches dried until it crested with hillocks. It looked like a barrow about to be exhumed. Its junkyard guts seemed perpetually disemboweled by street-people, their shopping carts rusted from endless quests for treasures.

Seventy degrees out. Get back on course or you'll be gone before the transients.

39

He closed his chafed eyes once. Forcing them open felt like ripping Velcro: Summer, 1991 AD, nightmares for real, the girl he loved dumped in a squat, the body stripped when he visited her that weekend. *They left her eyes open:* gored by fucks or rats. He knew what else had happened by the streaks crystallizing in her hair.

"Gina!" The noise made him shiver. It was a Puerto Rican kid yelling to a girl in a building next door.

"Gina, what I tell you 'bout staying up dere? Come down, okay?"

Giz couldn't stop himself from visibly flinching. The kid caught his shelled expression. "Hey, 'man.' Whatchoo lookin' at?"

Giz turned from the window and stared at the cluttered floor. Layered with papers dampened to translucent, the wood-pattern bled though like a contusion, reminding him of his own occluded pores. He raised his gaze. Cracked like a surface of a fragile skull, the white ceiling seemed ready to cave. Pictures formed in the ceiling's insomniac scribbles. He read a few morbid fortunes there, fissured with fault-lines of faintest ash:

Her slackened face, gilded to angelic, purified by shadows at sundown. For hours, he kissed the corpse and waited for dusk. Making sure no one watched him, he hoisted the body to its burial one block away. He dusted the rat-shit off her, dug into filth with wooden boards. When no one was looking, he stuck her down there—shit, someone's coming—threw stuff on top her, ran off, then crept back.

He told himself to avoid her smile, her stare. But his mind kept spitting wrong readouts like a tired hard drive. Hardcore loops of hands lifting the skin from her ass like the hem of a mini-skirt, ischium swiveling against cataracts of trash. Her face replayed in splintered plaster. A Nintendo labyrinth sliced open, its post-bomb graphics autopsied by overuse.

He was back in the squat, staring through Jill's missing eyes.

Clean off, little man. A shower would help him sleep. He walked into the bathroom, pulled aside the curtain and stepped in. The water hurt, at first. He watched the drops descend the tiling like deliquescent sperm. He couldn't seem to relax. He kept thinking someone was trying to leave a message on his machine. When he ran the water, he heard voices. When he shut it off, he heard his body drip.

He toweled off and slid wetly into bed, closing his eyes until his stomach burned and his chest went cold with panic. When he rested, the fear intensified. When he moved, it melted away.

Birds twittered. The bed felt like a queasily rocking boat. The only thing unfamiliar about the panic was where he felt it: rising like a puppeteer's fingers through his ribs.

He dragged his Proventil inhaler off the nightstand and took three rapid-fire whiffs. His body performed this act while he observed it. Like so many other acts. Like eating, like wheezing. Like his habit of blinking, once attributed to contact lens discomfort, now accompanied by a clenching of the eyelids—

RRRR-nnnnnn…RRRR-nnnnnn…

The phone drove high-end splinters through his nerves, so he rasped in answer. It was Michelle, Hiro's personal assistant from Worldfire, calling to book a Karaoke session. To Hiro, turning down work seemed implicitly disloyal. But when Giz tried to comply, he heard himself decline.

His call-waiting beeped and he answered someone else. It beeped again, interlacing his next conversation with yet another; then again, draining his spirit in a drawn-out suturing of the psyche. He answered each call numbly, his stray line caught in a fiber-optic gang-bang. When he hung up, the sky said *sunset*. Eidetic zoetropes changed to revelations.

Visions burned him until, spent, Giz finally closed his eyes. But even then, he slept in fits: caught in fistfuls of nightmare, brief claw-swipes at the sight of Jill's demise. In certain flashes, discolored porcelain fixtures swallowed her whole. In others, her plot off Third Street swelled to a crumbling tongue—steaming with heat as it licked away her skin.

This lasted until he settled into resting. Averting his thoughts, he sank to a final fade.

Counting the measures, he sang. *Counting the measures...*

Without past or sequence, the ride twisted out of time. The dream ate his voice. Its whims embodied him.

He dreamed of restlessly pacing through his loft. The window dimmed. He passed through a tunnel found between sink and stove, wandering into a vast chapel lit by a flickering kiln. The space resembled his high school auditorium. The floor gave way...

He dreamed of walking down Norfolk Street, where he met his favorite assistant engineer, Jared Singleton. Jared stood in front of his place off Rivington, an air-sign boho as lean as bleached mahogany. Trendy in dreads and velvet vest, Jared reminded Giz to book time for their project with Effector. *Just do it, okay?* Jared insisted with uncharacteristic harshness. Scratching his Jonathan Shaw tattoo, a band of black-lipstick lightning on his left bicep. Giz promised to book time for Jared at the Hit Factory. As he thought about music, his eyes relaxed. The horizon closed like a wound; the sky compressed to a low-lit ceiling.

Shit—he was awake. It was night outside, the darkness had erased his apartment. The clock's LED read eleven-thirty *a.m.* He felt for a jar, pissed into it and slumped back into the damp sheets. Upstairs, a Spanish family danced. Thankfully, the spell took less time to hold him.

He dreamed of recording vocals in Studio A of the Hit Factory, where he shared the desk with a shifting version of Jared. Sleep's void intervened, reworking the dream's coherence:

Giz asked if she could hear him, but the girl on the other side of the window seemed unable to nod, let alone reply. Jared, the genetic processor who sat beside him in the sanitized pink-lit control room, had rendered her mute by typing *Command M.* Giz glanced at the console: it was something new from George Martin Neve. The faders, the LCD, were indecipherable to him—as indecipherable as the record company's request that the artist show more subservience, more trepidation at the sound of her A & R man's voice. He didn't know what they meant by "a greater capacity for self-revision."

"I'm not sure what they want—this time," Gizmo said.

"*I* do," Jared said impatiently. "I've been on staff at A Mod for a fucking decade and I know *exactly* what they fucking want."

Giz forced himself to look through the glass. Imprisoned by biological complications, confined by insets of glass and surgical steel, the girl's throat was mottled with blue-black sores. The pulleys and pumps that scarified her lungs bristled with half-uprooted circuitry. She jerked as electrically enforced commands seared through her brain, through her limbs, through fissures in the Iron Maiden of her tendons.

His gaze climbed the glass, the frame, the flashing record indicator houseled in an interstice of white. Above these, the monitor extended from the wall on swivel-arms. It was tuned to the State of the Union. The President, an Alzheimer's-afflicted Republican whose rigid expression had worsened into ticcing and grimacing, read from his teleprompter as involuntary torsions slowed his speech to that of a dying vagrant.

"Take five," Giz told Jared. The remote was wedged between the desk and a strip of elbow cushioning. Giz picked it up and faded in the sound.

"We live in a time of political certainties......that just as surely as an artist portrays rape or violence in his work......he is inciting his audience to commit it......Metaphorical crimes are real, friends......De Sade's images of savaged chambermaids, of servant girls in leg irons, bind our American women even today......Let me re-emphasize this: ......speech is action......and fledgling rapists learn their *modus operandi* from books, television shows and films......The artist who portrays illegal acts should be punished with imprisonment......just as the woman who claims she has been raped should not gain a conviction......if the defense lawyer can show that she actually enjoys sex......This is because we, the ex-Calvinists of the right and left, make no distinction between rape fantasy and actual rape......nor do we credit the American public with the ability to understand the difference......That is why we must protect them from evil influences:......we cannot permit examinations of the demonic impulses of the id......though we do advocate an exchange in public debate:......questions of political responsibility for those of sexual decorum, resulting in an unexamined fascination with sexual scandal......then a transference of the public's responsibility for their own fascination, resulting in puritanical rage......"

Giz hit the mute button and paged Jared in the lounge. He hoped the girl would look recovered after the break, but she'd only continued her grim evolution. Feelers trailed from her temples, caressing and chafing them for the presences behind her reflection.

"She looks *bad*."

"Fuck 'er," Jared said. "I'll teach you to do this right, buddy—just like your first engineer."

"I'm telling you, man—the artist is always supposed to feel comfortable, but she can't even—"

"Don't worry, I said—I don't expect no credit in your next interview. Now watch this."

Jared touched the space bar on his keyboard and her head tilted forward, facing him like a de Chirico mannequin's. Arms braced against the console, Gizmo winced as he realized that *something bad* was about to happen.

Rising from toothless gums and bloody sockets, tendrils undulated with a circular motion that described *violations.* Invisible nails pierced her cheeks, crescents of sulfur burned her palms.

"Rachael!" he cried. Jared typed the command *Shift Reverse Birth* and her vagina muscles clenched on a zero. From the monitor, Gizmo heard a click and then a little scream. Jared hit the return bar twice, whistling as her womb was lacerated by spears of bone.

Giz woke clutching a knot of twisted sheet. He lay on his stomach in the glare of noon again, a pillow arched over his skull. The events of his dream shriveled until they became the objects which now pressed against him like eidolons of safety overturned: the bedding, the uninflected walls, the books piled chronologically from nightstand to disaster. None of these could negate the cruelty of his desire. *Am I fucking sick? Do I fucking come at the thought of murder?*

Light outside, and he wasn't afraid to awaken. Why *was* that? Oh. Oh right. That last moment of the dream—his eyes inside of Rachael. It made him stronger to taste that. The trance of empathy and the coma of the drive.

That wasn't me. The guy who hurts women, that was my dad, not me.

On his dresser tilted a little snapshot of his mother, framed and propped on an easel-back stand. It was signed *Eva Lake, 1985*—the year she legally changed her last name to erase his father's. She hadn't wanted to retrieve her maiden name. But she never remarried and refused to mimic the signature of her deserter: Knox Renner.

Giz never bothered to change his identity legally because

he didn't like to think about it. People knew him as Giz or Kevin Lake, simple as that.

My name is Kevin Renner.

An alias he was born with. A name like a jalousie against remorse. When the shame wore off, he'd call himself Giz again.

Inhaling the cool fluff of his pillow, he sheathed his complicity in the illusion of loss: *Poor Jill.* But it was small comfort to remember that the oneiromantic swirl of girl and engineer were his mind's pain-obsessed extremes—pos-neg poles of the sadism which, even now, Renner struggled to contain.

Vein Of Grace

From my untimely birth in the passenger elevator of the Hotel Clifford to my pre-trial detention in the Fairview Institution For The Criminally Insane, I have tried to lead an exemplary life. Having said that, I must duly note that all my attempts to act humanely have been mercilessly thwarted—firstly, by the petty cruelties of my family, who jeer witheringly at the smallest sign of virtue; secondly, by the pernicious relapses of my many infirmities, among which, I am compelled to record for the sake of accuracy, may be counted akinesia, euthalalia, staphylococcic infection, Rocky Mountain spotted fever, meningitis, aphasia, gout, delirium tremens, lupus, hemiplegia, phthisis, emphysema, sinusitis, colitis, Bright's disease, diarrhea, constipation, pink eye, palpitations, anthrax, coronary thrombosis, boils, eczema, trench foot, rheumatism, asthma, distemper, bipolar disorder, migraine and cystic fibrosis, to name only a few. In spite of this demoralizing convalescence, I have tried to raise my sights heavenward; but it isn't easy to follow one's principles in the face of brutal opposition. On occasion, my physical and emotional frustrations have led to behavior which, though it might be considered immoderate or hysterical by the small-minded, was justly conceived and exactingly performed.

Rob Hardin

If it were not for my pathology, I might have been recognized as a confirmed moralist. (It was a neurologist and not a social worker who once called me "a *ticquer* of impulses.") That is why, when my therapist claims I lack remorse, I say it's my brain and not his bathos that fails me.

Before Haldol's green howl erased the music in my cortex, I never wanted to murder anyone. Tabloid reports of butchery elicited nothing from me but impatience; immigrants and women were targets to ignore. Just as I loved my cats unconditionally—for their delicate movements and mercurial faces—so I found people to be fairly agreeable (though certainly, it must be noted, more problematic than cats). That is why my addiction and not my so-called instability was responsible for the death of Professor Meisler. I couldn't have taken an animal's life, let alone my teacher's.

In my own defense, I feel obliged to recount the events that led obliquely to Meisler's death. To convey the full extent of the tragedy, I am constrained to dredge up some thirty years of history (all, of course, in exact chronological sequence). I take no pleasure in the explication of this arduous subject. On the contrary: I must note that at the mere suggestion of the intestinal fortitude necessary to complete this interview, no less than twelve of my severest complaints have relapsed into sinister recurrence.

In the year of zero-zero, I was barely twenty-six. A studious invalid who convalesced in endocrinological luxury, I lived a narcotized existence until the morning my father took away my trust fund. My pulse (which I later measured with a stop-watch) quickened until I had to grip the corners of my desk to remain standing.

Panicked, I took a cab to father's house in New Brunswick and rushed into his study. I asked what I had done to offend him, but he would not look at me, let alone formulate an answer. His eyeballs edged around my head until I vacated the nexus of his view's negation.

As I canted against the bookcase in the hallway—the

very bookcase that first stratified the heights of literature into my childhood's Olympus—my tactless sister articulated the reason for my disinheritance: "The door is that way, junkie."

I didn't have to consult a compass to trace my descent from fortune. I left promptly, pausing only to inform the waiting cabby that I couldn't pay.

In the months that followed, my exorbitant prescriptions dwindled as quickly as my bank statements. Through a last wave of mailings, I found an office position with my uncle Norman's pharmaceutical firm, but it didn't pay nearly enough to immure me in tinctures. The only *absolute* relief available was sold on the street. Green Dragon Memory Burn was the poison that chose me: a dealer installed a street-cast faucet in my head, making a crude sucking noise with his lip as he fed me my first flask of extracted brain fluid. Gasping, I basked in an oneiromantic swirl of endorphin-gorged memory; in intimations of immortality that were soon to destroy my life.

My father was not long in setting my uncle straight. When employees complained of my green pallor and vacant eyes, Norm fired me on the spot. I looked for work, but I lacked the habit of competitiveness. I tried to beg, but an impasse of pride perpetually stopped my voice.

My landlord finally proved I hadn't been keeping my rent in ESCROW, and that no repairs in my kitchen or bathroom were necessary. I packed my needful things into a suitcase and put the rest in storage; weeping, I gave my cats to the ASPCA.

Inevitably, my options winnowed to one. Freelance crime was my sole escape from homelessness and brain-withdrawal's depths.

Thirty years ago, one couldn't go to a filling mall to drink the cerebrospinal fluid of vintage brains: bought memories were scarce when the head began to howl. On mind-white nights, when my inner eyelids blazed green and the sky

49

pulsed with burning veins, I tried to forget the ache until I couldn't. Slowly, my jaw dripped foam from a foundation-smeared spigot gone dry as the smell of smoking rubber stung my nostrils. Just before my vision went hollow, I kidnapped a neighbor and clamped him down to a homemade brain extractor I made out of a wine press and a doctored feedstation. After I poured his remains into a sanitation pail, I left it outside his house for his family to discover. Then I sat quietly at home and waited. (Often, it must be duly noted, my rheumatism flared up after a particularly violent episode; and I lacked the necessary strength to confront an insensitive and subliterate community.)

When people discussed his death, I nodded politely and tried to appear sympathetic. Everyone knew I'd killed him, but no one ever told the police. For most people, inciting suspicion was an extravagance. They'd acted badly themselves too many times.

Throughout slow summers, people thought white nights were bad enough. But fools who claimed the worst was over fell silent when a CIA-Mafia *coup* proved otherwise. The gray-matter famine of zero-five hit America like a promise gone wrong: in a season of hellish hollows, money vanished and hunger carved an R. I. P. sign on emptied lobes. Everywhere, desperate people ate the feeble, the callow and the slow. I couldn't see that; preying on friends invited the vacuum of loneliness; emptiness, not hunger, was what I feared. Refusing to slaughter the tabby cats next door, I contented myself with extracting the sense-memories of their owner. (Who but the hungry—tabby or man— is likely to value the brain of a senile, friendless cat lady?)

When summer came, I worked odd jobs in the city. Private citizens paid me in dog skulls, but not enough to quiet the howls of a disinherited addict.

What kind of jobs did I work? Murder, tot-napping, community torture—nothing that paid particularly well. In those days, people weren't worth very much: in suburban spheres, the *nouveau riche* remained so poorly versed in matters of etiquette that it pains me to recall their brazen ineptitudes. Anise pastilles, Chinese button boxes and marzipan were tokens that free-lance extortionists rarely received, no matter how conscientiously they worked; and nobody *ever* cared enough to tip an assassin once his victims were dispatched.

In the summer of zero-one, I traveled incessantly. Just to keep the business fresh, I happened to pass through Portland, Oregon. Sporadic work led me to a suburb of Lake Oswego, where one client—a stump-limbed, boil-eyed beer-tycoon—decided not to pay. All afternoon, I'd tortured his ex-wife's child as he sipped pineal gland extract fluid and simpered. He hadn't even offered me a snifter of dog-greens, so I wasn't in the mood for stories.

Oswego was a secluded place: a moss-blue clump of forest land with boat-houses and pampered adolescents who water-skied across a stagnant lake. I began to hunt for his burial site even before he said it.

"Fuck you, Spigot," he was shouting. "You *liked* killing that little boy. You're nothing but a spigot looking to get paid for pleasure. Now get the hell out of here and be on your way."

"If I were you," I told him softly, "I'd keep my voice down."

"Why," he asked. "Don't you want the neighbors to hear me callin' you a spigot—SPIGOT?"

"Whatever you think is best," I replied. Once the fun-house lens of withdrawal twisted my perception, it was impossible to see things clearly. Nothing I could tell myself would slow my spasmodic pulse.

The quadriplegic dead-beat stopped and glared at me in mid-sentence. My hand slipped into my back pocket. "Why do these *bêtes noires* lack refinement," I wondered as my fingers closed on the only sensible reply.

51

I hit him with my Ruger Speed-Six, spraying his face with a clipful of Plus P ammunition until it melted like a strawberry sundae. "How indecent of you to mention that a surgeon botched my cerebral tap," I said to a white strand of eyeball floating in the murk. "You see where it leads, calling sensitive people names."

By the time he stopped gurgling, my entire lower jaw was dripping with foam. Any local citizen would have had the capitol to avoid cerebration, so the neighborhood was that much closer to noticing the crudely installed spigot on the side of my head. With no extractor nearby, I pulled the remnants of his brain and sensory organs out of the murk and tried to extract the fluid manually. The process was slow and pointless. I've read that people used to juice brains that way in the Middle East, but I don't see how anyone could. In my ruinous state of health, I nearly passed out from the exertion.

I fed until the foam stopped flowing. Wiping off my chin, I realized that in a quiet suburb, citizens would pay close attention to gunshots. "You're not from around here," I could hear them saying, which always meant *serve when ready.* An untraceable stranger could provide rich fluid for a famine-crazed, ravenous family.

With the report of my Ruger echoing for blocks, a deliquescent corpse, and the smell of gunpowder in the air, there wasn't time to reflect on the decline of etiquette. I wondered how far the gunpowder smell would travel. Past the corpse's garage, I assumed, but not as far as the road. As long as I fled discretely, I had no reason to fear reprisals.

Thumb extended, I sprinted down the highway for a mile of drive-by dismissals. Deliverance came when a gold spray-painted vanful of ostensible drunken college boys stopped and its belly slid open. The moment I climbed inside, the van began to move. I couldn't tell whether pity or amusement had led to this act of altruism. Either way, I resolved not to disappoint my patrons.

"Dude! Where you goin'?" the driver asked brightly. "*We're* headed for the shore."

I glanced at him pensively, then smiled to the angular skin in the passenger seat. "Please don't call me *dude*. I've heard that in jail, dude means homosexual."

A fat boy perched on a spare snickered as he cooled his shaved scalp with an ale-drenched hand. "You must be really old, C. 'Dude' doesn't mean that anymore. And besides, everyone who isn't a Rightsider knows gays are people, too."

As their van picked up speed, I realized the boys were volatile liberal skinheads—*mid-skins*—who sometimes slashed provincial people for signs of unconscious elitism.

"Hey, look," someone said. "C's a spigot."

"Appreciate it if you wouldn't call me that," I said. "My name's Miles—Miles Weinhard, for the record. Remember it and we'll get along pretty well."

The fat kid continued to stare: his gaze flat, his lips pursed in a flounder-scowl of involuntary disapproval.

"Weinhard is a Jewish name," he said.

"It isn't Jewish, it's Norwegian," I answered with bruised politeness. "Not that I dislike the Jewish people." The fat kid shook his head mockingly as the angular skin snorted. "It's just that, A, I'm proud of my family and, B, you're mistaken."

"If you're Norwegian, why aren't you blonde," said the angular skin.

Don't show them you're sensitive, I told myself as I leaned back on a toolbox. *They find out you're sensitive, they take you to China.* I smiled shyly and pretended to study the exit signs. The skins went back to discussing their heroes and the music they liked.

In those days, commercial music was largely corporate propaganda. Naturally, when kids hunted through garage sale bins looking for juice, they *inhaled* old pictures, videos and compilation CDs. They needed to find glitches of truth that slipped past bureaucratic eyes: indications that syncretism existed before America's aesthetic went hegemonically unreal.

But when the mid-skins praised neo-spigot bands like Spume, and swooned over that "simple, honest one-prong music from the Heartland," I longed for a tonic and Dramamine. "Really," I said, after several minutes of uninformed condescension. "It isn't good to talk that way about the Heartland." The fat kid snickered, and my fingers closed around the Ruger's grip. *Did they think me impervious to ridicule?*

Then I saw The Dome, a cerebrospinal feed-mall in the shape of a human head. Fish-eyed, famished, I gaped at addiction's fata morgana; I'd never seen a giant skull before, but there it was, sprouting quads and veinage like the lode that squats on a victim's bulging neck.

"Huh," the driver said as the van creaked to a full stop. "They gots some weird amusement parks in this state."

"I'll get off here," I told him. I knew what the skull meant intuitively; the proximity of Green Dragon made me so desperate my jaw nearly foamed again.

"Good riddance," the fat one said. The van's rumble climbed to a grinding squeal as its taillights disappeared behind a curtain of dust. My eyes teared slightly; after checking my pulse, I wiped away the moisture. I couldn't tell which had caused my physiological reaction—dust or insult. I'd already decided to be thick-skinned, but the effort grew easier when my eyes returned to The Dome.

The first Dome was a gigantically enlarged cast from the skull of its late inventor, Doctor Luther Maphead Kennedy. The homage was slavishly reverent: below the giant skull depended a three-yard placard inscribed with characteristic Maphead sayings, such as "ALL EMPATHY IS EATING," and "A BRAIN-STEM DRAINED IS A MEMORY FED." In the interstice between pedestal and placard loomed the Doors of Reception, arm-thick entrance gates roped with textured polyurethane. Molded from synthetics the color of dull bronze, the details of their assembly-line stamp had been darkened with lacquer to simulate antiquity.

If the artistry of The Dome attracted me, I am compelled to note that my hunger alone reeled me in. I don't remember *deciding* to walk up the red steps, nor to pass through the Doors to the Cleansing Lashes—those rug-shreds of blonde-edged brown writhing over air jets, like the kind that caress a windshield in a car wash; I don't even recall *willing* my legs to sprint down the green mall to the GrayMart entrance at the end. Nor did I acknowledge the civility of the salesgirl who handed out axes as I walked inside. The howling grew to a point where nothing else registered.

This Way To The Feed Emporium! proclaimed a queue of signs prominently hung from The Dome's ceiling of chalk-arteried bone. Quickly, I hastened through the mall. No one knew of the killing in Oswego, I told myself. Yet hurrying through the pulsing gray corridors with increasing urgency, I felt as if my hunger had become posthumous—as if my desire to feed were itself suicidal, and my very proximity to satiety marked my intimacy with death.

En route to the store, I saw a shriveled homunculus hobbling toward the same destination—tentative in threadbare tweed, his skull frosted with a silver crew-cut. There is something succulent about a mask of cartilage gone papery with age; the occipital's thinning coffer of bone suggests the fine maturity of its fluid and the tartness of the pungent meat beneath.

Like any sensitive person, I resolved to allay his suffering. Tracking him from the back only, I presumed my lowly victim led an abject existence and would thank me for his demise from the vantage of his afterlife.

I grabbed the fragile octogenarian by the shoulders, then bashed in his skull with the heel of my axe. All tension and distress were lifted from his shoulders; the very muck that gushed from his supraorbital ridges seemed suffused with spiritual animus. *Blessed are the meek*, I managed to whisper through tears.

Self-sacrifice renewed me: I checked my pulse, which had subsided to a serene sixty. Cleansing my palate with tongue-swill of wasabe, I walked my gerontological delicacy toward a median arrayed with richer brains. Certainly, the mall's security team had witnessed the assault that flickered across their array of monitors; but I never went to jail for human shop-lifting, let alone for the withered man's murder.

Before I entered the Feed Emporium, I arranged the body—a doormat with legs—at its threshold. I kept the head face down to avoid the recriminations of its canceled eyes. My pulse, I am compelled to record, had quickened slightly; but as I passed though the glowing green walkway, I grew as peaceful as an exiled monk returned to his calling at last.

That store was the strangest medley of museum and mall I'd ever seen: high oak shelves and bronze placards on one side, stacked bodies and Three-For-The-Price-Of-One toe tags on the other. The aisles were mahogany parquets; nascent women promenaded down the aisles, opening glass jars, plastic-wrapping the pickled brains inside, and dropping them into big canvas carts. Singing in glee-club harmony as they tossed the brains from girl to girl.

I knew the dance was part of a promotional campaign for the dome's green-ribbon opening, but something about it frustrated me: the proximity of capering girls to fluid and prime cut brain. I don't know where I got the image, but as I watched girls playing catch with tins of Green Dragon and fistfuls of pickled gray matter, a picture came: of prison inmates flinging bile and feces against the bars, until diametrical streams mingled in the center aisle between cells. When the image faded, I realized the girls were *marionettes*—trepanned automatons hard-wired for simple choreography—pithed of wit for the transports of déclassé gourmets.

As I crossed the center aisle of the mall—an aisle embossed and burnished like the deep oak paneling of a study—the glow of a smoldering sunset drenched my vision. Without my lithium and Haldol, the *ticquer's* mania came: mason jars caught refracted light, their surfaces igniting with yellow-blue bands. Brain fever struck flash-fires in the shadows, until the entire length of the mall gleamed with deletions. Shrieking, I looked down: my arms and outstretched palms, the bare trunk of my torso and the feet I could barely see—all were immersed in the apex of a blinding green blaze.

Security guards gathered in the doorway, glinting like lead soldiers as they nodded and conferred. I lifted my axe into the air and began to hack at the glass:

—Explosions of gray matter, juice and jar-shards, splintered in sunlight, whipping the faces of attendants with blood and fluid. I no longer needed to feed at the flaming hub of the Dome: drenched in memory's flesh, I desired the distance between fluid and feeder to be their mixture. Recorded by cameras, displaced by restraints, my convulsion was a somersault into hunger's abyss—

The guards led me into a holding cell's supernova. White light from a window fed into a lake of flame.

The oblong pills they gave me said *Watson 387* on the side. I fought guards' hands; then, blissfully, torpor came.

In repetitive dreams, I continually swung my axe and obliterated the row of brain-coolers. Sprays of juice drenched every woman in every aisle. Each time the guards hauled me away, my belly sloshed with cerebrospinal fluid.

Eventually, the angels invaded my reveries. Sopped in sunlight, wilting in olive-gray sharkskin, they measured my pulse by the clock-faced skull of God, who leaned toward me woozily from an electric chair suspended from the clouds—a candy-striped straw protruding from a hole in his temple.

I must have dreamed of its heat for hours before waking in the sojourn of a feral sun. Guards heard my moaning and roused me; hectored and hung over, I was brought to the line-up room, where neighbors of the quadriplegic eagerly picked me out. They had discovered his corpse in Oswego minutes after I'd left and identified me as his worker from a mug shot.

I can't remember much of my later humiliations. For the next few weeks, my numerous neurological disorders mushroomed into full-blown Korsakov's: my memory's splice precluded days of pain...

...Randomly, I recall a mob of kids with equal signs razor cut into crew-cuts dyed red. They pressed flushed faces against the passenger window of the police car that escorted me to the Clackamas County Jail. Just as I was about to be pulled bodily from the car, a riot squad saved me...

Then came segments of withdrawal in solitary—my mind vomiting light into memory's mineshaft—followed by an h-bomb in ultraviolet: the sun's brilliance, which raked my eyes with sallow nails of noon.

My trial was a blur of fast-motion film, a live-animation short-short on the celerity of rapid-fire reprisal. The prosecutor was swift, the jury and judge malicious; my mental clarity returned only in time for my sentencing. In passing, the judge mentioned an irony which had not been cited by anyone in the media, nor for the duration of my trial: through dental records, the homunculus whom I murdered in the mall was identified as my literary professor in college, the esteemed and brilliant Professor Meisler. This blow to my heart was more than my conscience could bear.

I never denied my other crimes, nor did I feign insanity in order to be declared psychotic—though the judge was quick to exhibit his contemptible knowledge of psychology in dismissing me as deranged. But Meisler's death remained the only killing for which I was never charged— the insensitive and ill-educated judge actually deemed this soul-destroying crime *trivial.* "He was only an old academic," the anti-intellectual judge sniffed. (And a living compendium of destructive ideals, I gathered from the judge's offended scowl.) "The other victims were corporate men, officials and illegal meat. As for the professor, we're best rid of his kind."

Overwrought, I rose. Vividly, I recollect standing in front of the jury box, my fever's light bathing the courtroom with Last Supper effulgence. "I am innocent of all other murders," I insisted with Franciscan forbearance. "You all know of my various complaints—thrombosis, Madagascar hissing cockroach fever, radioactive contamination..." (Here the judge banged his gavel repeatedly, interrupting my confession with characteristic superficiality. My pulse, I quickly noted, climbed to a perfect eighty-four.) "...and so on. My state of mental and physical dilapidation, it must be noted, speaks for itself. But never in my unjust and exsanguine life did I willingly murder a superior man—an aesthetician, a scholar, a man, in short, of rarefied sensibilities. It is *you*, not me—*you*, the judge; *you*, our callow justice system—who ought to be prosecuted for this criminal neglect of humanity and culture..."

Without shame, I must report that at that point, my voice deserted me. Weeping uncontrollably, I fanned myself limply as my six-foot-four frame collapsed against the defense attorney's desk. The face of my pithed professor rose before me like a lavender moon; so bleached, so boundless—so raptly attenuated to Pater-like observations of beauty and delight; so keenly, pristinely, impractically pure...

Briskly, the judge gave me a life sentence without parole. I tried not to imagine the Solzhenitsynian tortures that awaited me; though rusted handcuffs chafed my wrists horribly, and the sight of an indifferent court reporter in sealskin loafers aggravated my duodenal ulcer, I walked out of the courtroom without a twinge of bitterness.

Rob Hardin

Unmercifully, my only mentor was dead; but for me, the gravest debasements awaited my imprisonment. Though I'd expected jail to be claustrophobic, nothing had prepared me for its kennel of crawlspaces; for its virulent swarm of surgeons in criminal seclusion. No cell proved safe, no corner private: often, when a frail man was brain-raped, retarded sociopaths looked on—aroused by screams, leering at his tears of interminable torture.

I was one of the weakest: like a pronoun's vowel, my failing vitality paled. My pores, brains and ass—all were ripped open until body and being seemed a wretched skin-thread stretched between holes. After years of suffering, deep memory-lapses became my only source of escape. Shredded by forgetting, ruptures and lesions widened into a single contiguous space, where I remained effaced for decades.

Within my cells, I looked for solace—but no proof of spiritual pardon ever came.

Beyond the vacant face of Luther Maphead's New Phage Penitentiary, dome-life imprisonment is futile and friendless: any gang of thugs can drain you, because cells are unwatched, and because our Zen-perplexed warden observes the practice of selective non-interference.

Which is why, compelled to transcribe these events and to convey my ordeal with the most extreme and exacting exigency, I note that in begging for death, my pulse and temperature have ascended to their pinnacle of pitch. The world whitens and the memory galls. The past itself becomes more pain than place.

No longer content to dream of geotectonic freedom, I wish not to escape this jail but to desert the world. Locked inside three cells—in a chamber of bone in a vault of stone enclosed within borders of blindness—there is nothing for me but to die. Still, my jailers watch me too closely for suicide; like my father, these callous bureaucrats will not entrust a soul's destruction to its hypothetical owner. I am my prison's Count of Monte Cristo; my only prayer of escape is in my *billets imaginaires*.

If anyone within feeding distance should read this shut-in's confession, I implore you: please erase my stile of misery. With pity, I pithed my abject victims; from whom you may consume, I address this last plea for peace. I wait for the day when a boy will disembrain me; when an Oedipus Rex will drain away all waking. *Bash in my skull and say it was self-defense*: if you, ideal reader, impersonate my son, I promise you'll find the role a ditch of riches. I buried my extractor and sweetbreads behind the prison wall; only the killer who inhales my secret smile will steal the locus of that invisible grin. In all my latest years of lobotomized keening, no one has ever overheard the site and sign of my marker. I'll tell you now, if you'll only drench what's left of my mind in genderless death. It's an old wooden tombstone; the crayon epitaph reads *Right's Gone White*.

Until you kill me, remember my father's words, delivered from an electric chair of castigations: "Son, I tell you the wine of an ancient brain is the most valuable property to inherit. Everything you'd wanted to ask the deceased is explained by the final flash-back. All misunderstandings dissolve, leaving the matrices of familial failure. Then a thalamus smile suffuses you, if only for seconds. Wisdom outlasts the rush—I cannot stress this firmly enough. Whenever you savor an old man's thought, the taste brings a revelation. *Only write down his secret before the howling starts.*"

So much for virtue's thirst. I await execution by your compassionate hand. Now if you'll excuse me, it's time to take my lithium.

Duplicate Fog and Dresden Cerumen.

There had been a series of spectacular killings west of Newhaven. By all reports, the victims proved more than imaginatively disfigured: The textured palette technique by which their intestines had been rearranged to suggest *Satan Casting ET Into The Lake of Fire* were the subject of both critical praise and craftsman's speculation. How had the strangely anonymous murderer been able to make his parings in murk acquire such distinct borders? Of particular interest was his work in broken capillaries. Here the shadings of blue and red were so subtle as to suggest the airbrush work of Futura 2000 (an ancient LES artist whose techniques have been much imitated in these times of draftsmen automatons).

But after the telejournalist reviews and panel discussions thoroughly analyzed Khaki Cadaver 5, and academidroids were left to dry-hump its aesthetic until the skin had been worn away, the public's lack of interest voided the subject. There was something precious in the murderer's technique; it was too self-conscious; it lacked the bold, splashy manner that Americans love. Clearly, this was not the work of some up-and-coming mangler, some quick-and-dirty death-merchant, some rangy, doe-eyed maverick mainstream killer—but since forensic experts later determined that the murderer was an idiot savant, perhaps financial success were better left to those who would actually recognize its rewards.

Dwayne was a hydrocephalic millionaire who

had squandered his trust fund on musical dog collars. They'd arrived by the mobile-homeful, ritualistically daisy-chained to Victorolas. But when his brokers came to remove his sternum and optic fiber caps, Dwayne knew it was time to join RMSA (Retarded Millionaire Sexaholics Anonymous) or face a life of aggressive, monosyllabic panhandling. At RMSA, he met a friend who was to become the very apex of his sobriety: Onion, a mongoloid turpentine heir who'd spent his entire fortune on topless shoe-shines. Through the I-Can't-Count-But-There-Are-More-Steps-Than-I-Have-Fingers Program, he became a successful infanticide entrepreneur, setting up his own BabyHeadGallery—a name that reflected both the nature of the murders and the stunted emotional growth of the killers themselves.

(Tuesday, July 9th, 1985: was it something I'd said, or had the individual molecules of styrene in Molly's flaming plastic cup become volatile mutagens, altering her genes? Why had her lips stretched to seven-foot long cave worms that writhed whenever the CFA inspector passed? I tried not to feel personally insulted, but the vertigo and loss of memory caused by low-level exposure to polycyclic aromatics was getting to me. Hell, I thought, why not propose on my monomer-dusted knees, the surfaces of which were already beginning to pulsate with passion and deformity? But it was too late. Molly had already changed into a 350-nanograms-per-gram representation of the Rape Of The Sabine Women, rendered in hot pink fur.)

Privately, however, Onion understood the true reason for his success: his ability to utter wordless streams of syllables that reduced his clients to a soporific state in which they'd empty their wallets, drop their pants, and imagine themselves contestants on **Wheel Of Fortune.** For Onion's special episode, the usual wheel was replaced by a huge, proctologically-correct representation of Vanna White's anus just after sodomy by the entire executive staff of CBS. The inflamed areas were marked off in greed-inducing shades of olive and magenta, and bore the potential scores that a spin of the anus might achieve: sex with broccoli pulverizers, cappuccino sprinklers, vibrating swimsuit erasers—you name it.

The grand prize was this: The endangered wildlife species of the contestant's choice, smeared with Heinz 57 and slivers of pro- sciutto, and offered to him for ocular penetration.

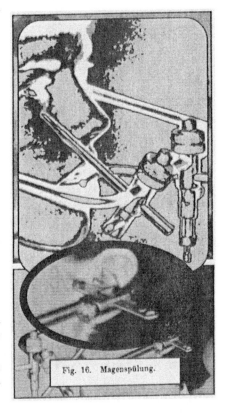

Fig. 16. Magenspülung.

65

*D*ressed to kill yourself.

The sites he recalled were sideroads of the broken. The faces of dispirited mobs, a drift-work of deltas—even the people he'd killed formed a discontinuous whole. It was a pattern he'd noticed before—though not until now with resignation.

Earlier that afternoon, the rest stops of the dead had merely seemed pathetic. Poor, puny things, he'd said, quoting Dwight Frye as he set fire to a corpse's hair. He'd watched it burn with something like aesthetic pleasure—the temples torch-maned, the eyes past all statement, like erasures. Then he'd doused the smoldering skull with Cabernet and gently placed it with the others. It was the zero-wide maw which topped a pile of severed heads so disfigured they couldn't even stare.

He'd stuffed the heads into a burlap sack and left them in Washington Square Park. He'd gazed down into the opening for a quarter of an hour, until blood and rot began to stain the fabric that had concealed them. Then he'd walked away coolly, feeling the heads settle and drain. An extravagance, he'd thought. Crushed peaches bleeding juice into the grains of white cobblestones.

Though he'd been wandering away from the death site for hours, William was still the unwilling recipient of

visions. The city itself seemed haunted, if only by emblems. A gangly blonde leaned against the support beam of the bus stop, her body a gesture toward negation. *Free me,* it pleaded. *I'd rather be dead than old.* Yet William rejected the corpse's luxuriant offer. Lusts sated, he felt free to reconsider fidelity.

Reflected neon signs hovered in cafe windows like superconductors of the unattainable. They floated beside him as he walked toward the Willamette Bridge. Even outside his mind, he lived in a city halved by rivers. At last crossing, he'd been sitting in his apartment. Then the phone rang. It was Katherine, the tiny speaker of the answering machine distorting her apologies into near-gibberish. She'd finally gotten up the nerve to call him and wanted to leave her new number. Instinctively, he'd risen from his seat, unable to sit or pick up the phone. It was all happening just as he'd predicted. After she'd panicked, after the infidelities rumored and real, she'd appeared six months later to ruin his dinner date at Hamburger Mary's.

And now she had entered his studio apartment through the phone line, her stammer tugging at his private face.

It was a voice that seemed too aware of time. Pitches came unmoored, syllables lengthened to slow tides. Explanations deserted the speaker, leaving dribbled ellipses, or consonants like sliced fingertips. It had only one thing to express—that hesitation had become the outline of the inexpressible—an aural watermark of Katherine's wordless fear.

Now it is midnight. His uneasiness recedes, allowing him to feel the night air. It sweeps across his face from the open window. He remembers paying to sit here—someone else's memory, a news clip he was too preoccupied to watch.

He sits beside a fat teenager with confederate flag patches sewn onto jean jacket pockets, confederate pins dangling from the sleeves. Did the boy sit near the black bus driver out of meanness or stupidity? The driver looks at the boy and smiles: *Racism rarely proves so properly labeled. If hatred were always that self-explanatory, one could*

keep perfect track of one's enemies—

*Demon-snakes
ate Dead Sea apples,
spitting bits
of bitter ash.*

William lifts his eyes from a page that smells of shredded coconut. They burned me with my own mind, he fumes. They always do. Like last Friday, when he'd attempted to get into Hellbound—a club known and reviled for its hostile door policy.

Tell them who you are, "Willie" Ross. Glare right into the doorman's squeezed eyes. Even if he thinks his position amounts to a royal title, even if he doesn't understand how power structures overlap, you won't have to cinch this guy a eulogy at tomorrow's wake. The people who know your name are too nauseated to slag it. They'll be holding back the syllables long after this current nest of celebutantes dissolves, and the club parasites have flitted out of town.

Forget me, Kath. I'm now a mere dead saint—a sinistral imp among Wilde's infamous loves. Condemned to endure the ripostes of yellow historians; born to imbue the dreams of Goths with black tears mascara'd on cheeks powdered harlequin-white, I trickle through currents on cirrus-shreds, bedding with scores of Beardsley's freak-show cherubs. I'm Everymask: I kill the thing that I love: I suicide to Berg, Hans Pfitzner or Christian Death.

A closet breeder who identifies with Gustav Allespach, a teetotaler pissed on opiates and downs, a privileged runaway reliving boyhood abuses, a pacifist who murders out of guilt, I photograph your hole for this alone: a living lens, now cleansed and culpable. I bow a *viola d'amore* attuned to tombs.
Here's what I do, he taunts in discorporate sing-song. I simply frame whatever can't be fucked:—

There were places in the Robbie Ross Memorial Cemetery that Albert lived to photograph. Often, his father would discover snapshots of tombstones mixed with those of the family album. Small wonder that Albert acquired a mortician's technique, smear-

†✕✖✠❖✖✦◆✖❖✠✖✕†

I am gristle. I am a masocide. I am a sprawl
(con-

†✕✖✠❖✖✦◆✖❖✠✖✕†

torso was said to conjure. Seconds later, a blood-vessel broke in

Headpieces of psychobiolog-ical driftwood are never al-lowed to recompose. They devolve on axes.

DeliriumTrampoline.
Slate-gray Bassinet on windowledge.

ing the lens with so much glycerin that even rotting cities were suffused with an incandescent vitality. His aim was to natural-ize Death's jarring detail; meanwhile, in Armenia, a statue of Achilles was discov-ered to have been installed in the wrong region of Kodaly Square. Rude folk music jarred the Apollonian sensibility that the Greek

Albert's jaw, spraying his gelid lens. This resulted in a final tar-nishing of the image: As stat-ues crack, so do aesthetics. Albert's last words pertained to the condition of his diffu-sion disc and not his "soul." Delusions of punity scorched his eyes, singeing the lids as cinders shrivel paper. They joined the ash of flesh that gathered along eddies de-fined by hills, rounding the veranda like nervure. Awa-kenings decayed in the silk pond: the fileted Muzak...

...in the individual can spumed illegal pesticides.

Though a mausoleum wedding dominates the opening scene of the romantic goth comedy, **Blurry Powder-soft Faces**, the bride soon exchanges suicidal vows at another kind of altar: the burning fuselage of none other than hemophiliac heartthrob Jeremy Plath. In a performance that is likely to land him this year's Sutured Smudge, Plath oozes liquid joy (and I don't mean the detergent). This film is not for everyone—"Insufficiently synthetic," one cadaverous fan was heard to rasp on her way out—but even so, sprigs of ammoniated tenderness alleviate the lack of repetition.

In one sequence, albino moth-people cocoon the dozing Plath and gaze at him with expressions of

heart-warming . . .

...nudity. Waif, degenerate, animated gargoyle spitting flecks of human skin—all were sketched with graceful touches by directors Milo and Otis. One wishes this sort of thing were attempted more often than the usual tasteless necrophilia that lurches through public access funerals and into our better graveyards. Forensics fetishists had better remember that the tomb is hardly the place for a one-sided fling.

†✕✖✚✦✖✦ ✦✖✦✚✖✕†
-tinued) whose last words are unimportant. If only (con-
†✕✖✚✦✖✦ ✦✖✦✚✖✕†

†✕✖✚✛✖✦✦✖✛✚✖✕†
-tinued) there were terms for the trace-marks of my fluids. Then I could de-fine the matter (as if it mat-tered). If only. Ne-ver mind. Nothing can protect my faculties from the repellen-cy of human contact. First, I invited the pathogenic embrace of the Body. Then I explored the hyper-stimulated minds of my generation, but that was worse. The interior of the skull is filthier than the genitals could ever hope to be. The eye in the window caresses the wind outside, and the tongue evokes its lewd itchings. This is what we call style, a toilet whirlpool of bad champagne which attempts to drown what we cannot digest. If only I could iso-late the illness. But when I try, my legs grow spattered with shit. Language be-comes a junkyard of slo-gans in which a gutted heart replays its craving for pain. Artifacts from the crematorium snake between my lips: vile inflections flecked with bile.

†✕✖✚✛✖✦✦✖✛✚✖✕†

IN THE GALLERY OF ILLITERATES

Awkwardly, Planer balanced his frame against the giant marble scroll, his head tilting into its whirlpool of furls. He was trying to look past the Hatchett instal- 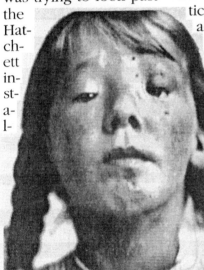 lation, a Plexiglas logo-griph of carnage, cormorants and giant tortrix moths. His attention snagged itself on talons and pincers— on torsos whose agonized poses were rendered abstract by their placement. The sculptures were enclosed within red Lucite brackets. These formed part of a vast equation of molded thermoplastic symbols that progressed across the gallery floor: pliant algebra notations, indestructible equal signs, flowchart symbols that opened enigmatically to the casual visitor beyond the gate. From the anticipated viewer's position, it was the Raphaelesque style of the sculptures that was foregrounded by their context. But from Planer's vantage point, the sculptures regained their urgency. Close proximity freed them from the ironic distance of Hatchett's age. That was why Planer found it so difficult to concentrate on the progress of the gunmen outside. He feared their approach because he knew they would give no pause for explanation. Excuses were meaningless to illiterate killers. Trained in the iconography of television, they could only read stereotypical body language. Once they'd closed in on the exhibit, Planer knew the gunmen would read him as an emblem of deceit. He would be accused and eye-tried with

one glance from their Emcee—then a nod would signal Planer's execution. He didn't anticipate remembrance or regrets. After they had killed, the gunmen instantly forgot their victims. Murder dwindled to slaughterbyte in their sequence of waking

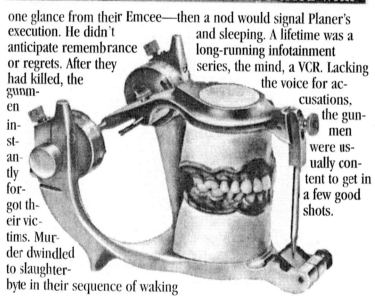

and sleeping. A lifetime was a long-running infotainment series, the mind, a VCR. Lacking the voice for accusations, the gunmen were usually content to get in a few good shots.

THE STAINED REMAINS LAY PLAINLY DISEMBRAINED

(or waned to flame-cerise.)

~~ρττψ~~ 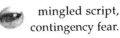 mingled script,
~~ρττψ+~~ contingency fear.

Her wet dreams glistened with slick-haired boys. They stood in

∀ΘΩΘ∀: ϑΘ≅∀
ΠΛ? *phhh*
ΨΨΨ*kkh:*

..η
ου
.ᛪ
∞..

oblique alley light, their Tenaxed razor-cuts framing thin-eyed derision. Heads turned slightly, girlish smirks twisted to depraved. A wind from

The reliquary possessed an air of disquiet. Presences blew through its halls like the scent of violent women.

nowhere scattered their denims.

Excessive lace entwined her thighs. Kinetic taws of Tiger's Eye retracted like the sacs of amber flies.

Torsos froze in profile, their icy erections nursing her desire until daylight shone through the brickface. Then the boys thinned to transparencies. Her dad's fingers reached through the loops of zippered legs and parted hair. Go away, she thought. Don't fuckin' care about me.

Astrosentics ascertained.
deliberations prove delaned.
Repentance crones cryonodrones.
Impaled, her veins lay famely unrestrained.
Ontologies decentralized
glean tart precisions wryly prized.
Tradition planes what film regains:the autononymic, frail terrains.

Then Dad surprised her. It seemed he wasn't so prim after all. When she ignored his commands, he pulled out a knife. He raped her there on the hide-away bed, thrusting the knife tang-deep into her left eye. It had long been his belief that pleasure and punishment must go hand in hand.

*Greased with leech's gleet, Houdini
proves last repast for Pasolini.*

Interrogator Frames

From the late edition of *The New York Times*, March 30, 1992:

New Nerve Tissue Generated From The Brain Cells of Rats

The adult mammalian brain, long thought to be incapable of repairing itself, possesses a pool of immature cells that can be coaxed to divide into new nerve tissue, scientists have found.

The discovery is the first compelling evidence that a mature brain retains the potential to generate fresh nerve cells—a talent ordinarily limited to the embryo.

Studying the brains of adult rats, Dr. Samuel Weiss and Dr. Brent A. Reynolds of the University of Calgary Faculty of Medicine in Alberta, Canada, discovered a hidden reservoir of cells that, when placed in a test tube and treated with a powerful stimulatory protein called epidermal growth factor, would bloom into neurons, with long, willowy tendrils, telltale signaling molecules and other hallmarks of nerve cells.

"It left us speechless," Dr. Weiss said. "We were trying to explain this to ourselves, before we decided to explain it to the rest of the world."

February 20, 2012.
SoHo, New York City

The afternoon sky was a lacerated painting of brain rape. It darkened with violet slashes, webs of black mold, pineal eyes. As Rachael stared at it, she tried to forget all that was mindlessly representational. It was as if the perfect, nearly intangible music of Josquin des Prez were

hidden behind a wall of cadaverous gurgling. She could-
n't seem to clear away the human appendages, the
semen that clouded the lens. Her ghosts had an odor that
would not be washed away.

The ceiling of the Neurolab hung above her, a viscid
overlay of pain that deepened as the sunlight faded. It
sucked her sex through holes that passed for shadows:
stigmata'd hands swallowed her thoughts, memory
wounds clenched to anuses.

She wanted to relax, as the doctors had suggested, to let
the embers eat through her. But the burn-holes widened
to ovoid screens—monitors in which fragmented scenes
repeated like ostinatos. Of her hourly terrors, she could
remember only flashes: the interrogations and the injec-
tions, the silver glint of the Knife Game. Then the flashes
ran together and there were no more words. All she could
see were green welts in a flood of stroboscopic white.

A blade slid slowly across her temples like the rail of a
boxcar closing. The strobe was burning out. Just before
glare switched off, a motto scrolled across the white hori-
zon: a brief procession of short, unreadable words. She
gibbered and the light cooled to violet.

By the time the sky turned thorazine black, she'd for-
gotten the pain of purple. Hours of narcolepsy gave way
to an idiot's twilight.

"Rrr...rrr...rrr..."

The sky was a millennium's mouth. A seamless shriek
of amnesia.

"Easy, Rachael. You're coming out of it." She squinted:
blank ovals shriveled to doctors' faces as the darkness
above their heads receded into corners. The night sky
became a spider web of cracked plaster.

"Can you feel this?" one of them asked. She couldn't. The
doctors glanced at each other and smiled. She felt herself
going under…

Fade to a waiting room suffused with tremulous light. The fluorescent overheads had a Parkinsonian intensity, their oscillations mirroring subtle brain trauma: failing synapses, petit mal seizures.

She surveyed the space and found she'd fallen into a white hole. No window, receptionist or patients. This visit, her company was reduced to the room itself: SoHo-open, its walls barely relieved by two studies in ink watercolored pale vermilion.

Can't take it, she thought. *I'm empty enough as it is.* Her eyelids fluttered in time to the flickering lights. Tilting back, she breathed—

—and pain emptied her skull. She convulsed, flopped forward, heard a stack of magazines hit the floor. Squinting, she confronted the double exposure of damage. Wreckage settled beneath her/an eidetic flashfire ghosted the office.

"*Help me*," she whispered. Amnesia swallowed her eyes. The pain receded to a hollow throb; her eyes relaxed slightly. The big analog clock above the door read 11 *p.m.*

Reflexively, she glanced at the sand-colored end table. No paper cup, no codeine, no Xanax 0.25. Eyes followed an oblique light source to the empty admissions desk: *definitely* no Xanax.

Familiar stuff: a sixties world's fair space-needle paperweight teetered uneasily on a stack of forms. A bronze placard rested on the edge of the work surface: *Dr. Reed Darmon, Ph.D. Ofc. of Research & Endocrinology.*

Her gaze veered to the television that gleamed in the center of the room. Usually, it was tuned to CBS. As she focused on it, the blue screen switched abruptly to a close-up of Dr. Darmon's face. His expression seemed less preoccupied than before she'd lost consciousness.

"Hi, Rachael. The growth hormone is working quite well, as you must have noticed."

Startled by his voice, she pointed to the monitor. "........."

Darmon smiled proudly. "Great, huh? Just got the system

installed. Now I don't even have to leave the surgery room to talk."

Flat stare, raised eyebrows. "Whattaya doin' up there."

Slight fish-frown as he dipped his head thoughtfully. "I told you. So...what do you think?"

You're creepier than guys at a bachelor party, she thought. "You've gutted my brain a dozen times and I can still think. Must mean something."

"Means you're a good test subject, Rachael. We pith your skull, the neurons grow back." In the background, she heard high, sleepy gibbering.

"But there's a problem 'cause like...I've been having flashbacks. The last operation...I remember it, even though I was knocked out. I remember the Knife Game."

He glanced away, then met her troubled stare with an expression of slight satisfaction. "Daydreams, hallucinations—all normal, considering. I wouldn't be concerned."

Knives are normal.

She faltered. "If you say so."

Darmon's smile tightened. The baby talk continued, beyond even the imitation of speech. Abruptly, it died. His smile relaxed to neutral. "I do. Now concentrate, Rachael. I'm giving you your money and your prescriptions..."—a scowl of concentration—"ATM-style. That's how it's gonna be from now on. Less contact. You understand."

A slot below the monitor glided open. She reached in and pulled out an envelope. "Shit I do to stay out of the business," she whispered.

"My best," the doctor said. His image dissolved and the monitor switched back to standby, eclipsing the screen with a visor of royal blue.

April 2, Greenwich Village
Her boyfriend's apartment

STONEWALL: 1969-2009, flashed a Christopher Street sign housed in shatterproof glass. Visible from Neil Renner's seventh story apartment on Waverly Place, the commemorative sign seemed the only landmark that had changed since he inherited the apartment from his parents. A jalousie of slanting architecture and fruit-haloed trees obscured all other street-level scenery. Everything got lost in the Caligari angles of the view.

Rachael knew. She'd been avoiding the sight for a decade.

His apartment looked even more cluttered than the scenery: a respectable space made shithole by years of neglect. The cream yellow walls and hardwood floor teemed with roaches. Tabletops mutated invisibly under heaps of moldering Chinese food containers, crumpled comic books and empty cereal boxes. His antique five-string Alembic leaned in the corner, a thousand dollar gift from a younger, stupider Rachael—out of its case so long the bridge wore a Fu Manchu of dust-strands. If she hadn't had to support the two of them, Rachael would have kept the place presentable enough for a Sunday soirée.

As Renner played with Beautiful, his pet tarantula, Rachael shook her head and smiled. It was weird to see this droopy, pallid white guy in his thirties, ring in his nose, flexing in 505's and braids two decades after the fashion, playing with Beautiful like a preoccupied, lonely child. He loved Beautiful because, like him, it looked mean but proved harmless. The venom had probably been removed from both at birth.

Beautiful disturbed Rachael—mostly because, aside from Rachael's store of self-directed venom, the two of them had so many things in common. Dark eyes, cryptic cast, legs as expressive as fingers. A habit of clinging to Renner and caressing him at the same time.

She and Renner had too much in common with Beautiful. The difference was, she fucked Renner. And he never hurt the spider.

"When you gonna move?" she asked Renner finally.

"When you go back to dancing," he said, opening his collar so Beautiful could crawl inside.

She drew back. "You want me to?" *Today, I made three thousand dollars. Five years ago, I'd have shared the money with you.*

His face aged suddenly. "Not here. Not in Jersey. Not in fucking Nowhere."

"We could move in with *my* parents," she said bitterly.

Smile-lines appeared on his face without any perceptible change of expression. "Let's not go over that again, okay?" he said quietly. "Just please calm down."

With a deprecating smile, she shook her head. "I *am* calm."

He raised his hands frantically. "Okay, okay, you're calm. Now listen. You know I'd never consent to living in Irvington. With your mother. Or the *asshole* who fucked you up." He turned and looked out the window, revving up. "It took you *so long* for you to figure out why you were doing it, dancing, all of that. The fucking masochism of it. And now you—you have a really good job, and the people hired you for your natural intelligence, and when *we* fuck around, the traumatic shit's exactly where it should be. Whereas that *asshole...*"

She wasn't listening anymore. No matter what he said, she was still supporting him after a decade. He was still a deadbeat who'd let his girlfriend become a lobotomy volunteer before finding a job himself. Yet here he was offering armchair psychological counsel. Like that was compensation for all her damage and toil.

"Yeah, we're a *lot* more healthy than my dad, Renner," she snapped. "Just shut up and make me remember why I'm with you."

He stopped fucking around with Beautiful and looked at her. "Nobody talks to me like that."

She smiled at him, catching the signs. "I know, baby. That's exactly what I like to remember."

They'd been playing with knives for hours, until Rachael's tongue was numb with the aftertaste of tarnished steel. Then Renner took a hit of whiskey and carved a zig-zag on her inner thigh. The wound was stylish, like a Beardsley asp. It darkened to red, then brimmed until he leaned over and licked off the excess. She was so fascinated that she temporarily forgot she was in pain.

Loss of blood made her eyes flicker shut. "Orange," she muttered.

He froze. "Huh? 'Orange?' You want me to stop?"

"Naw, forget it," she whispered as she fell off the edge of the world. "Pain's not bad when I'm asleep."

She woke in overcast light, her wrists restrained. *Oh goody*, she thought. *Renner's so wonderful. He knows when to slap me around.*

"Know what I wanna do?" As he stood looking down at her, she couldn't read his eyes.

"I can't tell." His smile was cryptic, his goatee the pivot of a question mark.

"This," he shouted, pulling the knife out of his pocket.

"Oh, you mean, mean bastard," she pleaded. "Not the knife!"

"And this!" He plunged the knife into the base of her skull. *Snap.* As she gazed up at him, brilliant lights surrounded his head, igniting his goatee with white fire. "I'm not worried, Rachael, are you? Like the doctor says, your brain always grows back."

He slipped a blindfold over her eyes. The shadows massed to black. White embers dimmed until she was left with an eidetic overlay of filaments: staircases made from the bones of birds.

When she tried to think, the darkness became unbearable. But when she stopped thinking and felt, the sense of isolation fell away. With blindness came familiarity; after several hours, her mind gave in. Opening to the darkness was like being a child in Daddy's lap.

"Here I am, Rachael." Renner slid under her softly. "Daddy Knife is here."

Wrists roped to the headboard of an old rocking chair, she slid down on him as he comforted her. She was safe in his arms, safe and degraded. His lap was a storybook with a dragon at the edge of the page.

Until she felt the knife. Renner wasn't using it, but his ghost was. The overlay returned; dead neurons were haunting her skull. Raking the barricades of an almost empty mind.

Viscid sky. Afternoon. The roof of her mind was the Neurolab ceiling. Stupidity closed over her thoughts as Doctor Darmon sighed, rapt in the intricacies of the Knife Game. She felt the pull of negative wind—the wind of the wing of imbecility.

Fuck Daddy Knife. Daddy was an asshole. "Orange," she said.

Renner froze. *"Huh? What?* But I'm not hurting you, Rachael."

"I said *orange,* motherfucker. Untie me *now."*

"Okay, okay. What the fuck."

"I wanna play a new game. It's called Knifey, Knifey."

"Rachael, stop."

Fuck you, she thought. The neurotic repeats a behavior pattern without ever remembering.

"The only way I can stop is to remember. You'll help me, right?"

"Of course I will. Anything."

She grabbed the knife. "Then sit down and shut the fuck up. Don't you ever think about anyone else? Or what I do for money, what poverty's done to me? The stripping and the prostitution? My life as a lab rat? Well, I'm gonna show you, okay? This is how you burned me, Daddy Sex and Doctor Knife."

"Rachael! Ahhh!"

"Hold still, baby," she whispered as she cut him. "I wanna show you what it's like to lose your mind."

She remembered the scalpel's progress by feel. A twist to the right erased the childhood. She'd lost hers several times, but it always grew back. Though lately it flickered like the light in Darmon's waiting room.

A twist to the left obliterated self-recognition. He jerked as she slid the blade through his skull. Now he was slumped in his chair, a man whose body had forgotten its own reclusive posture.

Shift shift. It was as if Aubrey Beardsley had drawn a study of an autopsy. Light and shadow traced the simplification of an interior—a serigraph, a cartoon.

In this solarized video of glowing ink and stroboscopic white, Rachael slid away from the body, remembering the purity of possessing a pithed mind. Nothing survived the knife—she knew it from her dreams of idiocy, from drooled valedictions and gibbered attempts at prayer. There was only an electric hollowness, more vacant than the emptiest room.

Because Renner was living in the hole, he didn't even know he was there. The abyss was an integer blurred. Skip, Skip, One, Two. Knifey, Knifey, I Love You...

Perhaps she'd leave him like that for an hour, then crack the door before sensory deprivation set in.

Like hell, she thought. *I really opened up to this guy. And he's still hanging around, just to prove he loves me. I told you they were out there, Mother. There are guys who'll love you even after you've carved out their brains.*

"Renner? Honey? Are you in pain, dear? Do you need me to wash your wounds?"

"Rrr-rrr-rrr," he replied.

"That's how I feel sometimes," she said as she stirred his brain-gook. "Like nobody in the world will ever understand."

"Rrrr-rrr-rrr...rrr-rrr-rrr..." He was a gibbering idiot now, as she had been when she lay on Darmon's table, or gyrated in go-go bars, or moaned in the porn world's valent void.

But she didn't feel guilty. *I take no pleasure in the Knife Game,* she thought. *If Renner hadn't wanted to be trepanned, I'd never have done it. He just needed to relinquish control.*

She pulled out a syringe. "Look, Rrr-rrr-rrr. Growth hormone. I get it special from Doctor Darmon. Believe me, your brains will grow back."

"Rrr-rrr-rrr."

She gazed at him mistily. "After a while—after you've gone through this a few hundred times—you know what happens?"

"Rrrr?"

She stirred his gook. *"Permanent memory loss.* You have all your motor coordination, speech, shit like that—but you don't have a past!"

"Rrr-rrr-rrr."

"Just think, Rrr-rrr-rrr," she said as she hugged the idiot. "No dysfunctional childhood for either of us. Thanks to Doctor Darmon, we'll be the healthiest couple in the world!"

"Rrr-rrr-rrr," the idiot gurgled. Rachael couldn't tell, but she thought he sounded more happy than confused.

Definitions for the Dungeon

on renunciation & aspirituality

·Epigraph on page iv of Sade's dictionary—forged:
Language is the hostage of the nerves.·

1. Bodies

Level 2: fingernails
Their function is protective, but their effect is to *confine*.
The Imprisoned would like to peel them off & experience
total nakedness, but pain renders this wish impractical. The
conditions of embodiment *dictate* that (s)he must live &
die in a straitjacket of overlays: the limitations of the flesh
are accentuated by the dividers which flesh *itself* must
wear.

As with the fingernails, & the rest of the body's bondage
gear—its visors & helmets, its shrouds, peplums, enamel-
ings, stitchings, & the dead-end apertures of the penis &
navel—so (s)he sometimes feels h(h)i(e)s(r) thoughts to be
lies, & h(h)i(e)s(r) lies to be fixed restraints. Like embodiment, existence is a state of *dishonesty*—the feeling that
(s)he is suffocating within a *second body*.

Level 1: history: death is all we remember
History is like a 3-D postcard—its depth is an illusion.
Because it is literally the organizing principle of a taxono-
my of rumor, history must be interpreted sequentially: it

evokes rather than embodies the centuries. Yet we often mistake *emblem* for *essence*; a chronology is wrongly identified with the stretches of time from which it has acquired its data. When we imagine history to be a trope for endlessness, we are misled: it cannot "immortalize" man's pointless struggle with nature any more than a sonnet cycle entitles the loved one to "live forever." The very continuity which history seems to record is as undetectable as a vampire's shadow.

Level 3: afterlife

The body glistens. Its flesh is hard, bloodless, & shiny as polished abalone. As the wind caresses the untenanted skull, filaments & hair catch between its teeth. Stains lengthen along translucent skin. Restlessly, it calls to its departed mind. It wants to twist on boneless hips—instead, it feels hot breath & hoots of laughter against its genitals. So long, someone whispers. Then a door closes & it is left alone with its separateness, contorted & desolate in the dirty hay.

Purgatives

Inquiry is the Catechism of the sadist. Deprivation is the Eucharist of the slave.

2. Cutting It Off

Writing

When writing seems poised like a window between reader & speaker, its opacity is gloved in a veneer of transparence. Inevitably, our eyes begin to sting from the effect of reading, as though the page had gradually become, not a portal, but a mirror which reflected the sun's white glare. This paradox is not ambient but unintentional: by scrawling runes on sheets of synthetic skin, the writer tries to *convey* but cannot. He wishes to delineate the conditions of his imprisonment, but only succeeds in vomiting—like the fly—through his appendages.

Irony...
...spoils expensive words with irrelevant overtones, undermines *ad hominem* morality, & submerges the listener in speechless passivity. It demonstrates language's inability to look at a thing & *call it by name.*

Sighing
Hanging from dashes, weighted with italics, the utterance caves in like the armor of a hollow scorpion. There is only the mind—& therefore *nothing*—beneath.

"Music doesn't have the power to express anything."
Only detached composers—like Stravinsky—are capable of interpreting our displacement. They *translate* because their language remains incorruptible, wordless.

Murder
Bodies are tools. But the idealist who uses them must eventually realize he *cannot* reach the outside, that he can't even communicate his lack of emotion. Having attempted to interpret the Other—bodies—with his nerves, he discovers perception's incoherence: its flickering linkages, its synaptic failings. Tissue is a filthy lens, & to live is to flail at intangibles in the soggy costume of a manatee.

Like Pollack, Masson & Van Gogh, certain artists grow convinced of failure: frustrated, mute, they are compelled to slash their canvasses. It is the same thing with the artist of the body: mutilation becomes his last vain attempt at transcending captivity. He slashes his wrists because he cannot escape his prison. He slashes the bodies of others because he cannot penetrate his prison's walls.

3. Barricades

Pity

I am often the conductor of a train which opens its doors to no one. It stops before the desperate crowd; I nod sympathetically to people who hurl themselves at the doors; the train moves on. The promise of warmth is a placebo which, though unreal, may be used judiciously to heal the sorrows of Others.

Recoil

I gaze distractedly at the summer sky. Like an impracticable rule, doubt slides over the view; it leaves me detached, sequestered by an inappropriate sense of *how things are*. I imagine that the world evades me.

Distant blasters argue, mothers trade insults in Spanish. My mind floats like smoke across a chessboard. Suddenly, I am literally *captured on film*: unable to enter the scene, I find I cannot move outside it.

Identifying with my body, I am unable to die; confined to existence, I am prevented from living.

Emotions...

...are too insular to share. They flourish in private: like illegal stencils, like penetrations, they slide from sheet to shadow.

In the movie house of the emotions, the present is a vintage print of a silent film. & the Imprisoned is the epileptic who slides to the balcony floor—existing elsewhere, gibbering.

Jealousy...

...is innocence: the Othello who lacks faith in his own allure is only too willing to trust in Desdemona's. Far from cynical, his emotion is naive, since it shows he trusts in the imaginary; his persistence in it is proof not of jadedness but childish trust, since *persistence* involves the repetition of an earlier impulse, & *to err* is to misunderstand.

Dreams...

...dissolve, leaving the memory cryptic, *disquiet*, like a de Chirico landscape. Only certain bland details remain, jarring the dreamer sufficiently to suggest an insidious context. Because they warn that consciousness might still be imprisoned, these traces expose the eerily *routine* quality of an oppression which—even while awake—the dreamer strains to perceive.

4. Büchenwald

Stranglers

The pseudo-Epicureans of the business world are oblivious killers—sleeping assassins who are programmed to strangle the very artists they profess to admire. Their purpose is to enact the death wish of the utilitarian executioner we call Nature. For like yon Cassius, artists think too much to reflect Nature's dead stare. They must be systematically destroyed by those who love them, like doomed animals hugged by the idiot in **Of Mice & Men**.

Neo-puritans

Without permission to investigate sexual borderlands, the castaway must abandon his compass & await the hearsay of unimpeachable authorities. That is why the neo-puritan rises to block the path of Defoe's explorer: his word must remain uncontested. The call to morality is a screen that conceals the writhings of Oz as he changes from the cloth of a minister to the leather drag of a dominant. His motto, which reads *The Rapture Is At Hand*, means to impeach the role of knowledge & welcome the reign of fear.

Satan

Preachers who dwell on the Devil's embrace are merely being possessive: there is a little Swaggart in every Reverend Falwell. The Good Christian who makes his failings wear horns is a moral transvestite. When a holy roller denounces Satan, he is blaming his self-hatred on a pair of red falsies.

The more naive a Christian becomes, the larger his devil looms: locking his door before watching **The Greatest Story Ever Told**, he feels the streets outside grow as sinewy & forbidding as serpents at the edges of medieval maps. The mythology of self-denial oozes from the magic box in his living room, & his glasses flicker like hearths filled with tepid fire.

The future

The future is a chromatic sequence of plumes arranged in the hand like tarot cards. It is an atheist with crosses for eyes. It is aerated beauty expressed in rude slang. It is the mottled claw that ascends a staircase of broken chords. We are standing at the top & wind has just ripped away the awning. We are building a gas chamber of contradictions & our blood descends from the gallows.

5. After Words: *Nothing*

<u>Epigrams</u>

In the reduction of tendencies to mottoes, & the distillation of attributes to definitions, the writer observes a single, amoral principle (this is my penultimate assertion): he follows the music of his tone in order to ignore the ravings of his "heart." This is because music is a diverting anthill, but revelations are a mistake. It is when you imagine you are writing your Credo that you unconsciously demarcate the cage of your distraction.

Writing/Recoil

…A Series Of Death Sentences

WRITING IS *dissonant counterpoint*—the chamber music of nightmares & empty attics. It is *vomiting* in order to savor last night's narcotics. It is contamination, the act of scraping pathogenic bacilli from the walls of the throat & injecting them into the mind of the reader. It is *recoil & distortion*, the sociopathic spewing of fictions.

WHATEVER I TRY TO SAY is negated by my mania to explain. It is this glitch which divides me. Am I the cartographer of vacancy, or a narcissist tracing his own reflection in sewage (language)? Am I writing an ode to sterility, or the self-summary of an absence?

WITHOUT INDUCTION, · my voice is impotence: it cannot recognize its captor. Was it you, *mon semblance*, who stretched me out like a hostage on linearity's narrow floor? Or does the fault lie with that doomed escape-artist, the subject? Suppose he shrieks, for example—if I attribute his hysteria to physical pain & then describe it, will he feel the discomfort? Of course not— my words will only create another paradox. I aim at The Father & succeed in blowing the skin off a metaphor.

WHEN NARRATIVE BECOMES A SEALED CORRIDOR with a pistol for an exit, the reader notices a breakdown in his identification with the narrator. Thanks to the writer, infection is inevitable.

WHY? HE IS LIKELY TO ASK. WHY AM I SUDDENLY REPELLED?

The pathology of the pronoun: *death, identity, writing.*

"I am a monster..."

What I ask of you is reasonable and moderate; I demand a creature of another sex, but as hideous as myself...

—Mary Shelley, *Frankenstein*

People, the monster began, are content to look past me as long as I don't open my mouth. But if I should say anything about the experiments that move me aesthetically, or describe the sound-patterns that float through my skull, the same people avoid my gaze with a visible, willful persistence. Somehow, I "throw" the ones I long to convince: I filch their focus, like a ventriloquist of souls. I throw and am thrown by their indifference. Their averted gaze is a white car that bounces me into some remote valley, where nothing I say can be measured or explained.

Day and night I hear the chatter of thinkers we've locked up in our bookcases, these ridiculous intellectual giants as shrunken heads behind glass.

—Thomas Bernhard, *The Loser*

Condemned to gaze at peers from behind smudged windows, (display case crystal and beveled lens) I consider the focal length of the measure itself, its averting valence. The space that encloses a rhythmic unit, a black anatomy, is always bordered by transparent walls. To exist between the barlines of birth and dearth—to *measure*—is to confine.

95

Rob Hardin

Shallow voices immure me in silence, a measure unmoored. Their owners prove thin in every sense: meager, unfinished, shelved. I have lived with their derision for decades and cannot help feeling defamed. Why do they slander me, and why must they laugh at me, why? Do they hate the invisible worm-wound in my neck? The beak-marks where the swan fed on the scarab larvae implanted by Pierre Boulez? I might bear scars, but I am no death-ward Grendel. I am not pathologically misanthropic or cruel. It is true that my father used to pull the hairs out of my arm when I misbehaved. It is true that my mother wept almost every day. But my aesthetics are not the result of abuse: I love *musik concreté* because I subsist on its pleasures. Yet I can't voice delight in a way that my peers understand.

As a child, my careful allotment of sound sources led me to calibrate dissonance like a pharmacist—to mix, to sift. My tapes of altered noise grew dense with revisions. By the time I rose from my secret operating table, a physician doctored, it was time to go to high school, where I felt even more reviled than before. When I became a senior in a Jesuit college, I applied my surgical tools to the body of the High Mass. My professors often seemed threatened by some savagery in me that I couldn't circumvent. Often, they revised and graded my compositions without comment. My asymmetrical phrases writhed in a second set of measures. Shrinking to subsets in red-pencil nets of corrections.

Years later, Mother mentioned that one of my composition teachers had referred to me as his only talented student. Hence my long hiatus under bookshelf glass. Now Saint Marks poets prove impatient with my quaintness; with my Latinate vocabulary; with cultural references that avoid pop culture and TV. There is a ghetto between the academy and the tavern, between the doctoral thesis and the cathode-ray tube. Karlheinz Stockhausen is the artist who led me there.

No one but me seems to retain childhood memories of removing the erase head from his two-track, of squeezing a cat in front of a microphone so that its mewling saturated a tape loop, blending with gasps, a harpsichord note, the din of a sibling yelling.

I have had to copy the name of Stockhausen's *Gesang Der Jünglinge* in journals for decades in order to realize I had habitually misspelled it *Gesang Der Jugend*. A sacrosanctity botched because I learned it so young and in secret. Misspelling my first love's name feels like my incorrect recollection of Hans Werner Henze's death. I recently made a bet with Richard Kostelanetz that Henze died in his forties. His life is so poorly documented that I cannot find any evidence of his death. Even so, I know he died in the seventies because I learned of it in my teens. I'm certain of it because Henze and Stockhausen were my only mentors. Misshapen marksmen who scarred me with Epicurean lead.

As a child, I was electrified by the experiments of postmodern composers; but in the words of Lynne Tillman, you can only shock yourself.

Even now, the shock stops here. I adduce their methods with disfigured lips, though none address my impulse to mutilate sound.

Always, I long to operate on speech. To interweave complex voices whose sexes and humanity I make unrecognizable with processing and blending and other refinements. I desire to make wolfhounds lisp at bitches and monks couple with nuns—not merely to blaspheme but simply to

97

alter their roles. I must make monsters out of talk because otherwise, my knowledge only mutilates itself; because the sampler alone can orchestrate my utterance. The mate I unmake is secondary to my final mate, its maker. Since I am floating in an insufficiently mutable culture, sound is my signal shot at entropy. Its synthetic tongue is my universal solvent.

My eyes trace the contours of stitched sound-events, visible landscapes, from my dissection room cell. I rewrite and refine images of my own identity until the idea of self itself proves too confining. I sew in order to break the stitches, like de Sade; to penetrate, like Michelet; like Bernhard, to push my forehead through bookshelf glass.

Avoid this gaze if you like, my hesitant hearer. Your silence frames new fissures through which to peer. Ignore the caterwaul of your captured echo. My circuit is solved. Your deflections designate space.

Syntax for Surgeons

As the minuteness of the parts formed a great hindrance to my speed, I resolved...to make the being of a gigantic stature...After having formed this determination and having spent some months in successfully collecting and arranging my materials, I began.

—Mary Shelley, *Frankenstein*

No one person has ever created a body of work...Only moments of genius from different people...can move an individual.

—Gary Cobain, member of The Future Sound of London

Timeline: 1993—Before Vintage Gear, Analog Tape, and Exotica Fetishism Revamped Frankenstein's Whipstitch as a Late 60's Antique.

Red Stingers Talk

Consider the milieu in which dead works remain written. The swarm of critics who tirelessly revise the Canon are driven by instinct. Their notions of purity erode previous ideas of elegance through methods more ancient than anything they intend to replace. Nevertheless, these imminent maggots, these agents of decay, must always rework the past they temporarily revive. As long as it stays intact, no corpus may live. You must sever a hulled thing's hand before it can move.

Now imagine an aesthetic world so redolent with whispers, a repository so packed, that silence and space drift apart like reservoir floaters. Rictal body and referent float side by side. Consider *daylight* as the texture of corpses wrestling, *nightfall* as stack upon stack of stiffs within and without. This rotting *entr'acte* pollutes the image of its witness. It demands not homage but vigilant depiction.

Like the critic, when the artist touches and retouches his queue of corpses, he *manipulates* the dead to choreograph the living.

> *Our concern is not with all monsters, but with*
> *chimeras, golems and Frankensteins:*
> *with monsters of translation and pastiche.*

Astronauts of the subjective, the romantics documented this bleeding of dead voices into the present with Zoroastrian precision. But as symbolism replaced allegory in narrative poetry, the romantic subject remained stratified on separate planes. Even when he wrote *Queen Mab,* Percy Shelley was not really free of the Platonic notion of changing versus perfect forms. Nevertheless, he constantly tried to bring the practical and discorporate worlds together. He did so roughly, by stitching his idea of the eternal to the framework of social ethics. He attempted to splice two worlds with the skin of the lyric.

In the egalitarian sense, he fudged the attempt. But artistically, he succeeded. Because his prosody thrived on breathless modulation, and because his rhetoric was in both senses sound, he forced heterogeneous ideas to cohere in air.

Shelley's methods had no small effect on his peers. After all, it was in his company that second wife, Mary Wollstonecraft Shelley, twice-failed creator—unwilling daughter-murderer and matricide—conceived the novel, *Frankenstein,* in which a far-sighted doctor combines the parts of several corpses to be shared by one reanimated brain. A hundred years passed before *mythos,* foregrounding only the doctor's demise, Mary's unhappiness and Percy's wasted grace, unburied the deferred action, the *praxis*, in the text. Just as *Orlando*, formerly an obscure detour in the evolution of Woolf's psychological novels as influenced by Strachey's translations of Freud, became the antecedent of magic realism, so *Frankenstein* proved the ancestor of postmodern aesthetics. In it, Mary Shelley forced life into her project—not into the novel-as-object, but into the *envisioned* artistic work to which the novel refers. As Percy forced his work to incorporate his ideas, so Mary's imbedded project is composed of heterogeneous elements. If Percy played Frankenstein, then Mary named him.

The *whipstitch*, a trope for the forced coherence of Percy threaded by Mary, loops into the present decade, mother to Stockhausen's *musik concrète*, William Gibson's cranial jack, Apple/Microsoft's desktop, the garrote-sharp sonorities of Industrial music, the choking loops of Trance, the flesh collages of Ambient House, and sutured misfit quiltboys like Robert Smith, Edward Scissorhands and Brandon Lee in *The Crow*.

First knot, cursed knot

Even so, the *depicted* whipstitch wasn't Mary's invention. It appeared neither in the original novel nor in the novel's earliest adaptation, a forgettable silent movie completed in 1911. The whipstitch *eidolon* was created by make-up designer Jack Pierce for *Frankenstein*'s most famous adaptation, the 1931 film directed by James Whale.[1] Whale's *Frankenstein* was influenced by expressionist films in general and Fritz Lang in particular. He wanted the make-up to reflect this expressionist bent. Pierce iconized Mary's pasticcio by taking the signature of an early surgeon's work—the crudely sewn overstitch, the suture linking one flesh to another—and making it the emblem of measures botched. Like the electrical storm that fed the

Rob Hardin

Jacob's Ladders on Whale's lab set, the surgeon's glitch juiced Frankenstein's monster to life, reanimating the dead green flesh of texts. In later films such as Corman's *Frankenstein Unbound* and Branagh's adaptation, the whipstitch reconfigured the lens itself (progenitor of pastiche): a track of threadwork disrupted the monster's eye.

Frankenstein's monster, Bellmer's dislocated doll

Green flesh seeded, aesthetics resewn. Take the surrealist game in which folds in paper indicate discontinuities in visi/linguistic syntax. Eluard and Breton discovered that folds between phrases indicated the artificiality of an unlikely sentence's construction, which rendered it strange and therefore vividly real. Arp, Tanguy and Dali used breaks in proportion and style to naturalize fantastic anatomies. (Deliberate crudeness, like that of a cartoonist who draws the smudge on the edge of a child's photograph.) Were the surrealists thinking of Mary Shelley when they named this parlor game the exquisite corpse?

The same stitch is present in music, from Strauss and Mahler's symphonic contrasts to Ministry's sampled thrash. Whenever the line between measures is foregrounded, the result is a sense of lexical rupture: a botched fermata, a clipped transition. An effectively placed discontinuity in sound. That rupture is perpetually underlined in loops, from rap to second century post-industrial to bands like Luscious Jackson, who pretend to play instruments even as the sound of their CD proves anything but.

The look of an alternative grrrl band, too, is an exquisite corpse. Each member is literally an appendage. This becomes obvious when a band's image is a trope on societal expectations. In their lyrics and performances, bands like L7 ("Let's Pretend We're Dead"), Hole ("Doll Parts") and The Breeders foreground the patchwork monster created by sexist expectations. But visually, they are examples of Bellmer's doll: the bound foot made willfully grotesque,

102

the whipstitched, recombinant ideal. In their videos, shots of soiled lingerie, sweatshirts and matted hair foreground emblematic bodies and illusionless eyes. Refusing to bathe, Courtney Love becomes the wet dream of outcast children, a doll which seems more tantalizing because it is soiled and twisted. The monster in danger of becoming another tied bride. A less fatalistic, Cobain-influenced diva, Kim Gordon manifests the doll in order to dispel the illusion. She throws shapes, as Thurston Moore might say. She traces the doll while swaying outside its borders.

Pre-Raphaelite John Cage on Ecstasy

As samples and loops recede into the macrostructures of multimedia and digital editing, the stitches get airbrushed, as in the music of FSO and Orbital (part of a trend in which Barthes's famous essay, "Is There An Author?," is adapted rather literally. The persona of the creator proves absent or unidentifiable in the work; audio/video anonymity is foregrounded to the point where the composer's absence becomes his most aggressive image.) Nevertheless, the sutures-and-all aesthetic of early industrial music tends to influence London's New Age Photoshop version of synthetic life. As in language poetry, brittle textures outstrip the purely seamless, which are only used to suggest the lack of any creator. The composer fears that people will imagine his samplers, computers and music history itself to be the true authors of his work, so he imbeds imperfections in order to affirm his presence.

Psyche Sutured

Physically, the monster is the result of appropriation, disjunction and lexical pastiche. But psychologically, the monster is expired film subjected to Lacanian mirroring.[2] The trope of the flaw is incorporated into his ethos. Self-knowledge is *permanently* deferred, in pointless search of a pre-syncretic context. Object relations are blurred by ghosts he

103

cannot trace. The monster is also clearly psychopathic, as evidenced by his narcissistic object relations. His lack of fear leads to a disinclination to learn from punishment. Perhaps his pathology is the direct result of another kind of patchwork monster, i.e., discontinuous acculturation:

> Children reared in a predominantly image-based, nonlinear, multimedia, briefly attentive society may not develop the deeper, unconscious levels of identity and meaning and therefore manifest a low level of empathy and a higher level of generalized anxiety.[3]

In the psyche of sampled music, the *whipstitch* is usually meant to suggest the grotesque artifacts that occur when man operates on the so-called machinery of god: when the damage is inflicted on the artist by society, making him monstrous; when the artist is perceived as grotesque by a monstrous society; or when the disgusted artist performs surgery, on himself or on society, in order to undermine the culture he violently opposes. Nietzsche, Hume and the rest have grayed out this last path in the Frankenstein matrix: Mary Shelley's idea of God presupposes that God is always already more than mere idea. Likewise, her image of a man-made, rational creation whose flaws have made him real is a Descartian take on the Cabalist's golem. What remains for us is Mary Shelley's sense of a flawed synthetic being—that flaws are what make the creature seem more real. Because he is an assemblage made from a microcosm of systemic expectations, the monster's metaphorical scale must be gigantic, and his defects must catch the eye before any smoothed edges. Because the spectator is tricked into focusing on the jump-cuts in the monster's body, s/he is less likely to question the proportions and texture of that anatomy's narrative. The monster becomes a way to naturalize the idea of aberrance.

The Everyday Whipstitch: A Practical Example

Today I bought a spiral notebook, the color of which I later found disturbing. Synthetic fuchsin green, its cover is intended to suggest the chlorophyll richness of moss and grass. Instead, its artificiality conjures a flood of Tanqueray gin bottles, fountain pen ink, Astroturf and plastic vines— as if through that fuchsin lens, all objects seemed nothing more than painted props.

With its impersonation of pool silt, the synthetic hue of my notebook proclaims the lie of the everyday. As long as I leave its surface alone, the cover smirks; its normalcy palls; it mocks the very things it imitates. But if I burn its edges with matches, tear its corners, deface its surface gloss, the cover warps, delivering its artificiality with surprising complexity and depth. The ghosts its color summons materialize with refreshing individuality. One apparition glares with empty sockets. Another reveals a dragging leg and sour smile. The lips are sutured, the arms, tessellated with scar tissue. Defiled, my cover-turned-skin seems a site for soaring eyes.

Is it possible to foreground the notebook's defacement until ruin becomes its most readable text? Every street corner in Manhattan shouts an obvious *affirmative*. An interest in man-instigated erosion is familiar to vandal, artist, professor and hybrid alike. The undertaker in us longs to dig right in.

Pretend I have just handed you a brand new notebook and that you, too, despise the color. You ask for the matches and set to work at once.

Minutes later, your notebook is charred, restitched, repainted. You videotape it, feed the image into your PowerMac 7600, translate the image's raw data into a soundfile and play it obsessively for your friends. A neighbor overhears you and deems you grotesque and sadistic, the Joseph Mengele of digital recording. You and your friends think this is funny and form a band called *Munich Humannequins.*

Now imagine all *sound resources* are notebook covers: smirking jingles and affected preacher's tenors. Through the use of a computer and hardware sampler, you have found a way to dismember the voices you hate. At first, you take a destructive, vandalistic glee in defacing the voices. Then ghosts touch their sound. Stripped of self-importance, the sound becomes resonant with deeper kinds of power. Like Max Ernst in his decalcomania period, you begin to trace hidden contours. You become Mary Shelley's doctor, letting your imagination and associative links dictate new structures beyond the naturalized. You visit a reliquary that wears a sullen, Edwardian cast.

You have just discovered the alternate world of the whip-stitch. Without even trying, you've made your very own monster.

Neo-Neo Industrial Technophage

The systematic dismemberment of sound is usually thought to be grotesque, a commentary on the grotesque artificiality of modern society, or both (as in Oliver Stone's massive sample playback suite, *Natural Born Killers).* The remnants of Whale's neo-expressionist Frankenstein haunt such technophilia. In the forties, the mere utterance of the name *Frankenstein* invoked terror because of its barbed, Germanic phonemes. Frankenstein's use of corpses reminded people of the experiments of Nazi doctors. That is why early technophiles like John Foxxe of Ultravox made technofetishism a trope for decadence and perversion, while their view of their own bodies and of society felt as chill as an anaesthetized lab rat: the desires and self-loathing of a closeted mutant. As if machine-fucking were the final unnatural act.

No Time Like The Present/Time Feels Like a Preset

The same holds true for techno, industrial and dark ambient. Unless it results in a soft-edged, streamlined, conventional object, the systematic mutilation of sound is seen as sterile, perverse and fetishistically grotesque. That is why proto-industrial bands like Einsturzende Neubauten and SPK flaunted their German aesthetic like a Blacklips performance hair-whips a crowd with peroxide. From postpunk on, bands grounded their aesthetic in Nazi hospital imagery, which repelled and attracted their audience. And as German expressionism is proto-industrial, so Trent Reznor reacted to this ideologically conformist, MacKinnon/republican world by invoking James Whale again. His video for the *Natural Born Killers* soundtrack is a montage of insects, machinery and butchered pigs, full of homages and borrowings from Survival Research Laboratories (Mark Pauline), the Mütter Museum, the Quay Brothers and Joel-Peter Witkin—all of whom share allegiances to Whale's *Frankenstein* with their dust-rich textures, romantic edges and fascistic, modernist machinery. Whale is indebted to *Metropolis* and *Caligari*. And Whale's film is itself a Frankenstein, a literary/cinematic centaur of modernism and romanticism. Whipstitched into being by *mutilation*, Mary Shelley's living revival sign.

Blood and Void

None who have nuzzled my cock survived the cost of that privilege. An erection is far too fragile for scrutiny: It swells with every sympathetic sigh and wanes to wilted beneath indifferent stares. A Jekyll-Hyde projectile skinned at birth, a face twice made Manx-naked by morphology and mutilation, my prick endures more pain than even pediatrician's scalpel inflicted. It feels without seeing. It wears its nerves on its hood.

Always, my family delighted in subjecting my second head to nettles. Father and Sister mocked it deflatingly, their roars suppressed to snickers at my sex's expense. As my tormentors knew, the boy who feels is flayed. But every familiar who ever scarified my nerves has died twitching on a homely davenport or easychair, with innards restrung like assets in secret accounts.

For six rigid years, I've knotted the prod my father mocked. Nights, I shift against my mattress, praying for detumescence as red glass razors carve the ghost-faces of my desire. I awaken from sleep shielding the rived eye, my anger's wound. I rise to silence werewolves and south-mouthed girls.

In all that time, no scraper has escaped—not even in spirit. Those who tried remain trapped: their keening devoid of voice, their howling tire-screech high. Stoned on vanity, such souls underestimate my indifference. My love is callow, a dicked stiff toes no conscience.

How do I find them? Let me count the lures. Trapped by tact, they shrink until I strike. Sensing unrest, they recklessly drink to Shiva. Lonely, they open, confessing to sanguinary setups. I'm always patient with those who hesitate. Beyond trepidation, I tenderly mislead them.

As I mislead them, so they go: in faith. The threat of death is hidden by their pride. I approve of the loser's instinct to conceal what's naked: loss. If truth be known, I'm rather shy myself. It's always better to be vile than visible.

Prodded to prowl, I find the Predestined snoozing in suburban dens and bedrooms. I brace their slumber with a come-rag dipped in chloroform. When they wake in a shielded strongbox out of state, they ante up; if I uncover a smile that chills, I appear the soul of sensitivity. Charmed and cornered, the loser wins one stab at redemption's exit: I show what has been scalded.

If ever I found one grateful face, I'd tilt its chin toward anger's exit. But the eyes never beam to see. When the watcher begs for deliverance, charity's mockery is veiled in every whine. *You deserve worse,* I think as my hook slides home.

Tumescence lifts this muzzle to corneal level; the hostage's retina dilates, until hole gives entrance to whole. Pearl spatters porcelain, cortex, bone. Rinsed of being, the spectator-skull rolls downward, an eye unpithed of vision. The clutter of the personality, voided with sight's last thrust, is scooped up briskly and lobbed into the darkness.

If my eye's skull is a spilled bowl, then what I see is the tear it briefly contains. When my lids close, my heads are emptied. No living thing can witness my nakedness. Stitched shut, the pig-pink earl is purged; hooded, my sex is safe, padlocked in parentheses. (Its lid's incision invokes the end of vision.)

Later, I crane toward light. We merge unpurged. I touch the blindness in this glare, holding its hotness in me till we

burn. As anger chooses, so I sentence the unsexed dead:
With dignity buried, or downcast eyes displayed. Whatever
you've seen, I say, I take from you.

Lifespans curve between my ribs like the dicks of men
on whom the crawling infant (me) corkscrews corrected.
Release brings peace; purblind gestation awaits. Buzzing, I
drive past graves and smile without sensation—embodying
shade, possessing the dead's in mine.

Distanced, I unclench my jaw. Each time I grip the
gearshift, it feels more real. Sometimes, I park to write verse
by a gas station's glare. Sometimes, I heel to the freeway,
erasing lines in my head—where only my sex, the secret
gourmet, can see.

> You're over, Dad, though not exactly gone.
> My sister's rictus reeks like burning rubber.
> Feel how I've reamed her blistering kiss. She slobbers
> the proof—a pinhead, skinned—into smoking hands.
> Grazing her face, this prick's the invisible man.

> > For The Shoemaker—
> > an impotent child who nursed his knife.

111

Twenty Paradigms

I. Tell Kip and her odor to wait outside.

II. In order to stimulate the tiny red arrows which produce hair, the skull sometimes suppresses the electromagnetic impulses which cause it to steam.

III. Have you performed this delicate operation on anyone else in the malt shop, Haney?

IV. He liked to order his paperweight to expand.

V. I can't read the letterhead on account of those roosters and their corny Italian madrigals.

VI. Aphid hail, aphid hail, *Homopterae* in the local mail!

VII. The patient lay on her side, with lava lamps visible in the lateral cuts.

VIII. Phillipa was sometimes aroused by pictures of Jesus and Mary and Him.

IX.   Look straight ahead, Joey, so's I can examine your eyes with these miniature egg beaters.

X.   I want the kind of artificial leg that plays big band medleys.

XI.   Kandinsky's *Staccato Abstract* was painted all over the defendant's lit up and pulsating hands.

XII.   Don't be a soggy bullet hole.

XIII.   Though he whispered an infinite number series to himself, Renard couldn't ignore the suggestive posturing of the lawn furniture.

XIV.   You can't play *those* records because *they've* shed their grooves.

XV.   The scamp has a huge, briny trilobite she likes to hide in people's piano benches.

XVI.   White gospel music is the bedpan of piety.

XVII.   See, the reason old soldiers never die is, their pores got windshield wipers.

XVIII.   Cough and the ladder softens; itch and the eel recedes.

XIX.   Before you erase the stool pigeon, I'd like to squeeze his tabby cat rhythmically between these sliding glass doors.

XX.   Come here, James, and admire this tuna melt's formal beauty.

BlowHo

The city was a sitz-bath of Madagascar Hissing
Cockroach innards, of crumbling Pre-Ruskin brownstones,
of heat and sweat and mucous and yet it was too sterile.
The urban hotbed had strangled under Westchester weeds:
Flock by flock, Rainbow Gathering fallout got Jeffed by
Canal Street Cannons, as N. A. pseudo-bikers revved Corgi
toy Harleys in waiters' faces. Stockbrokers in graying pony-
tails reeked jalapeño breath as they Murphied squatters out
of homesteads.

Skinheads closeted receding hairlines. Rave smartdrug
dabblers got twelve-stepped by veteran chemists.

NYC became the real estate spittoon of stage-set
ambiance, white-washed local color, and all species of
scum that passed for picturesque to people who'd just
moved there from Binghamton. Week-old rat corpses and
phlegm flecked with Body Bag masquerading as Lucky
Seven ("In my day, they had *real* heroin") glittered under
the gazes of suburban college backwash and moneyed run-
aways, primed the business-bups-turned-weekend-bohos
who stood before gutters holding tarnished silver copies of
Trick Baby, chanting *yer disease is doin' pushups* and the
onomatopoeically-incorrect monosyllable, *ow.*

But Dude! listen, you gotta go to BlowHo, that's where
guitar-destroying, nightie-wearing, sexually indecisive para-
philes go to fellate unregistered shotguns, and don't forget

JoeToeHo, the community of artists that pronounces Giotto correctly, and then there's KotoHo, the Japanese Nationalist sector, and SlowHo, the ghetto for the musically impaired, and Throwho, where the bulimic masochists live, and Shrome-Ho, the foot fetishist contingent, and WhoaHo, home of Danny The Wonder Pony and the saddle he should clean from time to time, and FroHo, that sector of the village where aging semi-guitarists give blaxploitation soundtracks one last shot, and No-Grow-Ho, an economically and creatively ravaged uptown thriftworld Nuyorican neo-beats pretend to have visited when asked for directions, and Sko-Ho, where tease-haired skeeziks hang out at Webster Hall, hoping to do New York literally. You gotta go to the edge of the shore off Eleventh Avenue and gaze at the decaying fifteen-year-old hustler bodies locked in crack paralysis, their mouths open where they'd been blowing some panicky trick and froze on his I AM THE RANDY KRAFT PENCIL-SHARPENER SLAYER 12-centimeter erection.

Forbidden Mammal

The story you are about to hear concerns no one
and disgusts even me.

—Sgt. Schnell, *Top Coprolaliacs*

Squealing like a cartoon mouse, the churning teakettle yanked Jennifer's gaze away from breakfast. Swearing, she rose from her plate of chutney to grab a jar of Taster's Choice. Usually, scarfing a handful of instant coffee lightened her migraine, soothed her synesthesia, and drenched her thalamus with a profound sense of spiritual well-being. But today was different. Even a jawful of freeze-dried swill couldn't drive the mouse-shriek out of her thoughts.

Jennifer had two choices: Arrive at the office by seven, or ring the boss to tell him she felt as wobbly as a taxidermist who can find nothing else to stuff and begins to stare hungrily at her own legs. Common sense nixed the second option: She couldn't afford to miss a day of work. Besides, no one was buying her sick calls anymore. Often, when she alluded to her degenerative mental illness, the senior editor studied some region below her neck, pupils following an invisible ferris wheel. It was strange how easily she offended this man who always seemed to be staring at her breasts.

Better to show up demented than to call in sick, she decided. It was already a quarter to six and the train ride took forty-five minutes. She grabbed a tropical-vomit-orange blouse that seemed to suit her anxiety level, but-toned it with effort, pulled on the matching jacket and glanced at the mirror. Did she have any orange lipstick in her purse? Vermilion would do.

On the other hand, what if she had a cow in front of the boss? Could she really explain away another fugue? Probably not, she concluded, as she slumped back into her chair. Not since last Friday, when she'd screamed because an Eiffel Tower paperweight had clambered over to her desk, curving its point in the direction of her knee.

Stressed, she returned to her food and her reading, a fash-ion spread in an ancient issue of *Details*. The boys wore bangs swept past their temples and knee-length dresses that reminded her of kilts. Johnny Depp must have started the trend. She tried to imagine her thirty-five-year-old boyfriend, Hank Meerschaum, standing next to the beauti-ful male models. Hank was too old to wear his hair combed back—the wrinkles would show—and had grown so shapeless after his last bout with depression that it was dif-ficult to picture him in swimming trunks, let alone a gown. Maybe if he tried that new slimming gel they sold at the Greek Boutique...

That was the problem with pictorials. They made you lust after the people whom the fashion photographers and designers got to fuck. It was the same with cartoons. Just look at that succulent piece of tail, Minnie Mouse. Her ani-mators had had the hots for her from day one, Jennifer could tell. In early photos of Disney, she could see the jeal-ousy in his eyes—the same forbidding glint his underlings caught when Walt reminded them to draw Minnie nice. But when Jennifer scanned reprints of the earliest comics, she always found a panel in which Minnie smiled provocative-ly—sliding three gloved fingers across a furry leg like a pornstar mutant.

In later comics, the artists experimented with pho-tomontages of a rapidiographed Minnie surrounded by cut-out celebrities. It didn't matter whose faces graced her coterie. Whether the owner was Sinatra, Chevalier or Chaplin, each luminary leaned beside her, staring adoringly.

But for the real-life Minnie who moved the animators, day to day life was bound to be less idyllic. Had Disney compromised Minnie's damehood while promising to make her top mouse? Jennifer had her suspicions. And what if the celebrities who surrounded Minnie hadn't behaved so adoringly? What if they were mostly straight white males like the ones Jennifer had heard about in college? The depraved kind, who made snuff films and ran for president. Who violated Jessica Hahn in church-bought hotel rooms under oil paintings of a pale, oblivious Christ. Who sat around in den rooms, plotting to molest russet-haired girl scouts while bluffing at poker and puffing on phallic cigars.

Jennifer kept picturing Minnie's flapping red suspenders and rippling black fur, her modular ant-ass quivering in scenarios as numbing as segments on Court TV. Wedging her magazine place with a jelly jar, Jennifer scooted her chair back until it rested against the bookshelf, pressing her fingers into the skull-dents just past her eyes. She fought the vision bravely until her eyes crossed. After a session of prolonged squinting, only surrender could drive the mouse from her thoughts.

Her mind went dark, like a theater ready to dream. A sixteen-millimeter projector rattled awake. The screen flashed white; then film-edges and numbers snaked by so rapidly she was sure they had burned themselves into her subconscious: a subliminal sequence.

Soundtrack: a biker-fast graft of meringue and sixties garage music, strangely filled out by major seventh chords on a tremolo guitar. Like the crawls in sixties' porn films, a disclaimer rolled across the screen:

Rob Hardin

THE DIRECTOR WISHES TO STATE THAT, YES, SHE UNDERSTANDS
THE DIFFERENCE BETWEEN RAPE AND RAPE FANTASY, AND THAT,
NO, NOT A CREATURE STIRRING HER PHEROMONES, NOT EVEN
MINNIE MOUSE, WOULD WISH TO ENDURE THE FOLLOWING SCE-
NARIO IN REAL LIFE. HOWEVER, SINCE THIS NASTY DAYDREAM
REFLECTS JENNIFER'S DESIRES ACCURATELY, WHY SHOULD THAT
MATTER? WHY IS THE STEREOTYPE OF THE XYY GHETTO RAPIST
MORE OFFENSIVE THAN THAT OF THE INBRED RAPE-CRAZED
CRACKER FROM TENNESSEE? IS IT BECAUSE THE MYTH OF WHITE
SOCIO-ECONOMIC OMNIPOTENCE IS AS ACCEPTABLE TODAY AS
ANTI-SEMITISM WAS A HUNDRED YEARS AGO? SHOULD MY
MINORITY AND GENDER STATUS ALLOW ME TO CHARACTERIZE
OTHER RACES AND GENDERS IN RACIST TERMS? WHICH OP-
PRESSED MINORITY OFFERS THE FAIREST POINT OF VIEW? THE
LATINO TRANSGENDER MARXIST? THE HYPEROPIC INDONESIAN
CASTRATI? IS AN AFRICAN-AMERICAN SCULPTOR'S WORK MORE
DISTINCTIVE THAN THAT OF AN ASIAN SCULPTOR? IF SO, IS THIS
BECAUSE DEMOGRAPHICS FAVOR THE ASIAN? WILL AN INSULAR
LESBIAN SUPPORT GROUP OFFER IMPARTIAL COUNSELING TO A
SEXUALLY AMBIVALENT WOMAN WHO IS ENGAGED IN BISEXUAL
ACTIVITIES? IS CRIME PERPETUATED BY THE DEPICTION OF VIO-
LENCE, OR BY SOCIETY'S FAILURE TO UNDERSTAND THE FUNC-
TION OF DEPICTION? WHEN OPRAH WINFREY FOCUSES ON TEEN
MURDERERS IN ORDER TO DELIVER AN ANTI-VIOLENT MESSAGE,
HOW IS HER APPROACH DIFFERENT FROM THAT OF *MENACE II
SOCIETY*, A FILM SHE HAS PUBLICLY HELD ACCOUNTABLE FOR
INCIDENTS OF TEEN ROBBERY AND HOMICIDE? IS IT TRUE OR
FALSE THAT MANY OF THE ARGUMENTS COMMONLY USED TO
DEFEND MULTICULTURALISM CAN ALSO BE USED TO DEFEND
EUGENICS? DO YOU UNDERSTAND THE DIFFERENCE BETWEEN
PROPAGANDA AND SATIRE? ARE YOUR EYELIDS GETTING HEAVY AS
I WHIRL MY HYPNO-DISK AND COUNT TO TEN? I DIDN'T THINK SO,
YOU BUG-TORTURING, PHISH-WHISTLING, SIDEBURN-RAZING,
SUBURB-DENYING XENOPHILIAC PSEUDO-HOBOES FROM THE ME-
DIEVAL SIDE OF DENVER! THAT'S WHY I REST MY CASE-LOAD...

The screen crawl dissolved to a track shot of an unruly
stage. Minnie stood trembling at its center.

The scenario went like this. Incarcerated and held in a padlocked auditorium at the edge of Disney World, the swarthy, voluptuous mouse was charged with committing an act so blasphemous that its merest mention would corrupt pubescent Funny Animal fans forever.

Jennifer tried not to imagine the pandemic result: children plagued with a psychological affect that compelled them to masturbate over any toy or cartoon character with crescented pupils; an epidemic of crowded playroom orgies in which tots jerked off over Captain Planet action figures, Raggedy Pam Andersons and gingerbread Jim Careys, occasionally electrocuting themselves on the glowing dresses of Heather Locklear Angel Light Barbies.

Since Minnie had committed such a blasphemous crime, a hidden Disney Tribunal had convened to sketch her fate. On the strength of testimony delivered by an inkwell exorcist, the tribunal sentenced Minnie to be disciplined by a queue of puffy-skinned, porous, life-sized white celebrities. Ceremoniously, men in baseball caps and bunny ears carried her to the center of the auditorium stage, hogtied her paws, and bent her sideways over a cafeteria table in a position of primate surrender.

Though Jennifer felt perplexed, these mixed animal metaphors didn't seem to distract Minnie's captors. In the oblique lobby-light of the proscenium stage, the distinguishing traits of the despoilers proved easy to discern. Letterman waved a special pink cigar while Moe and Curly nursed each other's erections, scowling and giggling respectively as they watched.

That ever-paling flake, Michael Jackson, went first. Stage left, he moonwalked over to Minnie's behind, reached for her garter, unfastened it with his right gloved hand and snapped his own suspenders with his left. Squeaking, he pushed back Minnie's chintz tutu to expose her bottom, then moved his hands robotically to his hips and hat-brim. He struck a few jazz-dance poses, tilting his gangsta hat forward as he thrust.

He turned conspirationally to the audience. "Wanna see Goofy?" he stage-whispered to a row of fascinated children.

Spotlight. Orchestral stab. Michael froze, his hips moving almost imperceptibly. Gradually, his pin-striped pants slid to his knees. His erection inched its way into the tiny animal's backside, a tattoo of Goofy pulsating on its tip. Goofy disappeared into Minnie as Michael's frown intensified to an eighties scowl "Uh! Uh!" he squealed in a Diana Ross falsetto.

Stage right, William Kennedy Smith strode out of the shadows. Teeth clenched with nightmare preppy glee, he unzipped and immediately began chafing Minnie's larynx with his Smith and Wesson.

The trio moved in a *pas de trois* of forced penetration. Michael's thin bleached fingers gripped the mouse's tremulous ears while her throat constricted against William's ammoniated penis.

A warped recording of Mussorgsky's "Ballet of the Chicks in their Shells" began to play. An antique reel-to-reel slowed and sped up to match the rapists' fluctuant tempi. Jennifer tried not to hear Minnie's muted squeak as a volley of flute grace-notes punctuated each thrust.

When the two men finished with Minnie, they zipped themselves up and shuffled unceremoniously away.

The stage bustled with impatience and confusion. Who was next, the white males wondered aloud. Someone said Peter O'Toole, but the speaker proved to be a fraternity pledge who liked to repeat the actor's name in lavatories. *Arnold Schwarzenegger,* someone else shouted, but this was the vociferation of an Aryan exchange student who noticed that pronouncing the famous actor and eugenicist's name was a seemingly innocuous way to utter a bi-lingual racial slur. Coughing slightly, Minnie's father, Walt himself, emerged from the projection booth to take his place in line.

Jennifer's eyes fluttered open. Stinging and swearing, she lifted waxen fingertips from her *In Case of Medical*

Emergency, Check My Credit Rating bracelet. (Her palm bore deep red creases from clutching the plastic edges.) Reflexively, she reached underneath the table to tug on the elastic band of her panties. What was it about menacing straight white males that always caused her to masturbate? Did she touch herself because the insipid Yalies who wrote for the *Village Voice* practiced reverse snobbery against all examples of WASPishness except their own, and in so doing made WASPs more tantalizing to lovers of the forbidden? Was she compelled to wank because the media, the left, and universities everywhere had transformed white males into the Rich Zionist Devils of the Nineties, who always seemed ready to claim ownership of her *mons veneris* as well as her cash?

Hardly. For Jennifer, the attraction had existed from the beginning. The dangerous pheromones exuded by white males carried a thrilling, tacit charge. To her, every white male seemed evil: in possession of unfairly allocated power, so utterly, selfishly demanding when it came to servicing his pink, surgically exposed penis, that all she could do was lie back, allow her wrists to be red-taped to the bedboard and take it, take it, take it; to be cuffed to the backseat of the patrol car by traffic cops; to service the entire greedy, interminable crew of fratboys, presidents, Grand Wizards, stockbrokers, and policemen...

Jennifer crinkled her eyes and stared at the table. Her teacup had stopped steaming long ago. She tried to ignore the affected sing-song of the silverware. She remembered a line from Alfred Bester's *The Stars My Destination:* "taste was smell and smell was taste." How humdrum, how utterly tedious that book had seemed. She had spent the morning trying to forget the similarities between smells and sounds, and here came Bester to remind her of the truth. That's why she preferred more escapist stuff: Tom Clancy novels in which people moved and objects remained mute and stationary.

Through the slats of the white blind, the day began to brighten. The murmuring of the room descended in volume. Perhaps she was ready for work after all. She leaned back in her chair and yawned. The sensation was deeply satisfying, like the sound of the final chord of *Der Ring der Nibelungen*. But when her mouth had opened so widely that her jaw threatened to detach itself and slide across the floor, her satisfaction began to fade. Distantly, she heard the sound of the Enterprise shuttle doors closing. She tried not to picture Picard's skinhead rage, the über-Semitic cast of Quark's propriety and profile, Katherine Janeway's passive-aggressive hostility, or the sociopathic insincerity of Captain Kirk. But the pictures kept coming until she felt spent and impassive. She reached for the keys in her coat pocket and felt a dusty tongue caress her palm. She looked down at her corporate jacket, the white man's corset. She sighed—and as she sighed, she heard her pocket cough. A formal, whiteboy clearing of the throat. As if testing the mike, to make certain it owned her mind.

She eyeballed the stove and the magazine on the table. Fuck you, she said. Enough kissing ass to save my job. Affecting her pocket's cough, she called in sick.

"Mr. White, this is Jennifer Fuentes. I can't come in today because I'm having a really bad attack."

The boss clicked his tongue and the office came alive. She could feel the repercussions long after he hung up the phone. On her desk at work, inanimate objects arranged themselves into letters that spelled the name *Alfred Bester.* Deep in the art director's office, the One-Hundred-and-One-Dalmatians wallpaper growled at sniffed blood. And in the publisher's waiting room, an oil painting of Christ stuttered, *T-t-t-that's all, hoax.*

Tweaking, Jennifer stood on her chair and pulled down a ream of vintage Disney comics from the shelf. Minnie would understand. She, too, was the wiggly victim of patriarchs.

124

Punishment Masque

Lana

This is the glove of the interrogator, a ravensblack smudge closing widescreen over my eyes. Blindness is sweet, like a sunset dipped in treacle. I'm standing in the noon glare as he drags his hand across my face: zippered fingers, orange blood, a Jackson Pollack sprayed across the hood. He forces a pebble between my lips and I swallow gratefully because suffering is worship and worship is addictive. He says I want to be ruined; I dwell on that as he strips me. What I think is, I'm drawn to the morality of it; to the iron maiden of vice in a decade of paper laws; to the spear of sensation in a siege of fundamentalist decals; to the revision of rules that slip from the skin because no one in her Reich mind is going to mutilate the body for the shame of the soul.

My mind slips back to the reflector of my self-obsession: my savior in chrome, the Mirror Man. In the words of Dirty Harry, fuck me. Fuck my ID number, Mister Death. I can't explain about nothing, Joe, man like you in uniform. It is special man who dress like enemy.

And it's a quiet man who ropes me to the chair, leaving his questions unvoiced—so quiet that I have to tell him everything. I'm talking about you, Silver Surgeon, MD. You don't have to utter a sacrilegious word. You're already the priest of the Narcissus project, the flower-press of romance. There's nothing you wouldn't do for love or retribution.

Alan

Trampled bud, tubercular blossom. You are the bloom I eti-
olate, but I am the sun-plagued jardiniere.

*The only thing worse than the nightmare of existence
is the nightmare of existence fading out.* The sentence
thuds like a chord from *Salome*, looping in my mind as I
rise from sheets as damp as a human tongue. Staggering to
the bathroom, I'm thrown off-balance by the tilting floor.
According to the landlady, it buckled when the last tenant
started a fire in bed. I can't visualize that—the cigarette-
ignited sheets falling to the floor, warping it into an unbal-
anced deck. It's too hot to be picturing a death-blaze.
Ninety degrees out—that's what the radio claims. At the
end of spring, a Manhattan twilight burns like the before
scene in a beer commercial.

Lana

It wasn't always this easy to talk about the weather, was it?
You used to look so anxious when you pictured my pain.
But it's always the sensitive fucks, the guys who entice my
empathy, who hammer me to history's cross. What about
you, Senator Al Fish? Does it go back to your mother, your
sister, your aunt? What diseased matriarch made you lose
interest in women? Was it watching your father ditch your
moms in the Revenge Club that first made you hate the
words I-love-you?

Alan

When my aunt tells me she loves me, I want to rip off her
head and shove it so far down her neck that it lodges
between her ribs. This isn't the first time I've been gnawed
by her declarations of need. Only yesterday I made her
watch the scene from *In The Glass Cage* in which a child
is murdered with a syringe filled with oxygen. When she

tried to wrench her gaze from the screen, I held her skull in place. I warned that any attempt to look away would confirm her suppressed hostility toward her own nine-year-old son. Later, she had a dream in which she found a spider-web and I thrust her face into it. I told her the dream meant I was helping her to confront buried emotional trauma. What it really showed was the keenness of her instincts. I had recently been thinking of burying her alive.

Lana

Confused women cling to your sadism as if to an oxygen mask. Tense and pressing, their feelings encircle your personality until you become part of their emotional respiratory system. Unwittingly, you exchange your role as savior for the drudgery of an artificial heart—for a foreign presence that alleviates the sense of a hole.

They often grip you in the same way during sex: as if hanging onto a prosthetic self. They fear they are slipping into an emptiness which they'll later imagine to be their own lack of intelligence, talent or individuality. But the seed of trauma is buried pain. That's why their eyes cloud at such moments—they can't see the forecast for the tears. Rapt in their own transgression, they believe they are helpless; but you, my closet thespian, are the only one who cracks. The savior of the suffering becomes the renunciate of restraint. You dream not of pleasing women, but of seeing them die.

Alan

When I torture you, I'm not raping my mother. I'm resisting my sister. She was the invidious bitch who destroyed my childhood by exposing me to ridicule: by claiming I once had an older brother whom she killed. It was all an experiment, she said. A way to test the effect of shame.

127

Trouble is, I've never found my way out of the lab. Whenever I feel humiliated, she seems to carry my cock in a searing test tube. To wave the burnt prize in my parents' faces. To display each specimen from my file—each limb, each film, each flow of blood and semen—with an amateur surgeon's utter glee.

I never liked that clinician's home movies, but I do enjoy setting fire to the projector. My favorite reel is the one where childhood ends; the one where I say, it's time to pay for experimenting on my pride. I'm going to replay the moment you failed to kill yourself. When I visit you in the hospital tonight, don't feel ashamed if I marvel over your bruise-blackened face. Remember—I'm only here to do you one final, familial favor: to end this sequence of extra-curvicular concern. Just watch the bouncing ball, the seceding plug, the leveling meters, the flatline in green. I'm here to correct your mistake, Dear Sister. I'm here to help you die.

Lana

Maybe you don't really hate anyone; maybe you're not a cold fuck just because your ribs were barbecued by a psychotic sibling. Unable to trust your friends, you try desperately to despise your family. This is how it feels to fail, even at being a monster: like your county, like your bank, like United States Currency, which is stamped with the face of the father it betrays, you are headed for the frost on a bloody red sled. Stripped of power, lying face-down on a shatter-proof bed, you shriek at your sister in sexless humiliation. *Fuck off, bitch, fuck off and die.* It is cold inside your skull, but you are waiting for a colder November.

Alan

Then let me tell you about my wife. She wanted to take my picture, but I couldn't allow it. Sadists hate to be photographed—even when the object is to create a memento of torment for a narcissistic victim. Instead, I photographed her—so that she could look at herself and imagine the invasive touch of the invisible man. I identify with the director Dario Argento when he says that, in his *gialli*, the black gloved hand of the murderer is always his own. When a victim looks at a snapshot or a mirror in which she herself is slashed open, she should see only the tips of my fingers and my cock: never my eyes. I want to stay buried—tenderly, viciously—in her mind.

I secured her body to a chair with duct tape, which I also placed over her lips and eyes. She warmed to me uncomfortably, as if to a seduction. Amazed by my own dispassion, I concentrated on the aesthetic moment of her shame. Her skin grew flushed as I slid a guitar jack up her vagina. More jacks followed: down the sleeves of her corporate blouse and up her tan-framed ass. I didn't hate her, exactly. I even commiserated with her as I wrapped the cords around her legs and arms. "She" was loving it, but "I" felt warmth and objectivity at the same time.

I found a ball-point pen, hiked up her skirt, and marked off sections of her stomach, calves and pelvis: Section 1, Incision Line 2.5, Section 9: Cut here. She grew hotter still as she bonded to me, reveling in her—sorry if this sounds pretentious—climax of degradation. (I don't know what else to call these moments.)

After photographing the event, I untied her. Immediately, she seized the camera, saying she couldn't wait to develop the film. Yeah, I said. Me too. But I had no real interest in seeing the results. For me, the experiment was over.

Lana

Looking at these shots of your "victim," I click my tongue with disappointment. I'd been expecting an austere progression, but there's something touching about your photographs. They're like a record of a first date, or a suburban couple's hobby.

Your documents of "degradation" are the illustrations of your ambivalence. You can't care about people if you're this indifferent to their thirst for love. Love is the lie your "victim" tells her id because she doesn't want to admit her complicity. But *your* love will perish in an unfamiliar alley.

Your aunt tells me you're a misogynist, that you loathe women. But what if you were gay and treated your lovers cruelly? Would people wonder why you hated men? No— they'd ask a more pertinent question. They'd ask why you hated *yourself.*

Alan

"Myself."

Lana

Yeah, Mister. That's who I mean. Have you figured out what I'm asking? This isn't "an evening with the analyst"; you're not "the man in the snake-pit" who's here to be "cured" of "sickness." I'm hunting for the eyes behind the smudge, the leather sneer zipped open. Are you really as fair as you claim? You say you've always believed in the equality of women; fine, I believe you. The thing of it is, you don't believe in your own.

Do you really understand the phobias, the fetishes you've inherited from Christianity? Do you recognize the subliminal pull of early Newport billboards? Of films by Lynch and plays by Tennessee Williams? Doesn't it seem strange how Americans praise individual freedom while blaming their perversions on the people they desire? Is there any truth to this transference, this chain letter of condemnation? Are your wicked eyes responsible for my destructive cravings? Is a girl in a low-cut dress asking to be raped? Tell me another...fucker.

Me, I jeer at Sunday stand-ins. For outsiders like us, sex is a snuff film for hypocrisy—an all-American *Salo,* where the stereotypes of sin die in interesting ways.

The true punishment would be to *retreat* from perversion: to suppress how it felt to brave a parent's whipping for the sake of defying his will. To bury the instance of exhibitionism that preceded the sensation of shame.

That's why you're here. For you, sifting through my head is like being a prospector in a glittering mine; for me, opening the mine shaft dispels the fear. You explore my secrets because you'd like to enter me so completely that you touch even my past, my pain, my history. I expose your emotions because I love to watch the face of the invader. The ambiguities of power and helplessness require no script: to renounce control is to reclaim it. In our reckless attempt to live in one interlocking body, let's not sacrifice a moment of awareness to the clichés of bondage. I'll never lose my taste for submission—but neither will you, Mister D. You'll never tire of being unmasked. You love the searchlight of a blind girl's hand.

Twenty-Five Reasons For Liking Horror

1. I can't get it up until I watch a strong female character perform oculatio on a train of David Duke republicans.

2. Delinquents worship it for timelier reasons than those of critics who insist they shouldn't. (And we have sworn to imitate the behavior of teenagers without regard for personal dignity or prudent self-analysis.)

3. Blood is wet and gooey like sperm and meesure, isn't it? So getting it on your hands is rather like, you know, coming. I mean, I haven't actually killed anyone yet, but in *Texas Chain-saw Massacre Part II*....

4. Sociopaths get really far in the business world, and in these days of a failing American economy, it is important to study their code of ethics as often as possible.

5. Fictive blood-baths are healthier than actual blood pressure.

6. Mutilation is more beautiful than excess, Mr. Wilson—just look at the protagonist in *Crash!* or the guy with two penises in *ReSearch*.

7. Fingerpainting is therapeutic, and fingerpainting in red translates particularly well to film.

8. Supposedly, deconstruction equals nihilism and nihilism is dead. So horror, which can only be defended

from a nihilistic point of view, is dead as well. But deconstruction is concerned with avoiding phallocentrism, not belief-systems, and nihilism isn't any more of a terminus than Peter Lamborn Wilson's ethical credo, which he paradoxically calls "amoral responsibility." Nor is horror inherently nihilistic, as any reader of H. P. Lovecraft knows.

9. We feel this isn't an ethical dilemma, it's a fashion problem! The theories of De Man and Deleuze were seminal in the 80's, but any school of thought that prevailed in the last decade is always declared out of date for twenty years. So we have agreed to be secretly influenced by deconstruction while denigrating it in public—like Camille Paglia and every other hack who writes book reviews.

10. I like the part in *Reanimator* where the severed head licks the Dean's daughter's vagina.

11. A grisly horror film is indispensable after sex because it relieves frustration. (It is terrible not to be able to murder one's partner while coming.)

12. Horror films with female protagonists often employ a reductive process similar to Beckett's. All footholds of safety, all emblems of personal power, are systematically removed, so that the character's consciousness is reduced to a primordial state and, betrayed by external reality, turns on itself. This is accomplished with the same effect in horror as in Beckett—but in horror there is the additional virtue of *cheesecake*. We have found that the profusion of arsenic-pale shut-ins with brimming bodices, cowering waifs in lingerie, and near-catatonic swimsuit model survivors of atrocities in whom the fight-or-flight impulse has been distilled to a compulsion to shower, aid immeasurably in the digestion of Beckett's message.

13. Violence is porn, and porn is the head cleaner of the human mind.

14. Blood, feces, urine: if they were good enough for Pasolini, they're good enough for Americans.

15. All human sacrifice—even self-sacrifice—is made to the beast within. The impulse to kill is like the need to dream. Just as we must have nightmares to avoid hallucinating while awake, we are compelled to ritualize our violent side. Otherwise, health—ours or *someone else's*—will suffer.

    Since we feel the slaughtering of Christians is problematic, we do not recommend this Roman method of catharsis. Instead, we suggest that the Roman arena be replaced by the VCR, where the spectacle of human sacrifice can be simulated in as grisly and harmless a manner as possible.

16. I wanna be a good boy, but bad people make it impossible. *Punish them—punish the bad people!*

17. Really, you'll feel better if you just admit it—doesn't the plethora of class-breaking romantic comedies that tearfully emphasize classism, wacky-neighbor spoofs that place The Suburban on a pedestal of irony, children's stories underwritten for drooling adults, weren't-we-idealistic-even-though-we-now-feel-we-were-misdirected-and-refuse-to-leave-our-kids-a-margin-for-political-error 70's sagas, I-should-have-fought-in-Vietnam-but-didn't-so-let's-bomb-some-Arabs 60's sagas, thinly-veiled Teutonic commercials for the afterlife in which God is dubbed "The Force," and quiet-son-this-is-serious-imperialism-in-which-racism-is-superficially-confronted-and-all-the-white-people-are-embraced-by-wretched-foreigners-at-the-end adaptations of E. M. Forster leave you with an irrational thirst for revenge against the selfishness and narcissism of Upper Middle

135

America? And who is better equipped to carry out this revenge than Hollywood thrill-kill incarnations of Charles Starkweather?

18. The sockets of monster masks provide insufficient sexual gratification for the normal American male.

19. Beauty is numbingly smooth unless it possesses a flaw. That is why we are wildly attracted to the dismembered victims of John Wayne Gacy.

20. The eye is the window of the soul, but the navel is the hymen of the stomach.

21. It is difficult to name an instance in film or literature in which violence leads to complacence.

22. The body is a temple, but the viscera is a sewer.

23. If you want to master spirituality, you have to study the Aztecs. (The child is the father to the bleeding man. The Mother of Mary is the Son of Sam.)

24. Ever since Three Mile Island, radioactive parasites have been living in our brainstems. They gnaw at the limbic system when we write how-could-you-die letters to Michael Landon.

25. In the bestiary of consumer consciousness, there have been many stories about dogs—Lassie, White Fang, Rin Tin Tin. But only in horror films is homage paid to the noblest of God's creatures: the termite queen.

Death is Expensive

I relived "The Casque of Amontillado" as Paul Schaffer sealed in the secret bricked-over NBC elevator that had been used—fleetingly—by Toscanini. Bored, bald and feckless with celebrity small-talk deprivation, I strayed from the segue spotlight into that conductor's conveyance with only my cuffs for sustenance and my personal python, Bob, for company. Often, in my ensuing eon of need, I turned to my venomous pet for motivation. Where there's a snake, I reasoned, there's the crack of a Canadian chance.

Bob the Blood Python was five feet long and ten years old with a possible lifespan of fifty. Without my foley artist's gig on Late Night, I had less to live for than Bob—but that didn't mean I'd sub for his coachwhip's hors d'oeuvre. When fully fed, his temperament was phlegmatic; but after seven hours of florid muskrat deprivation, Bob proved too ill-humored for show tune snatches. Earnestly, I prayed that the overhead monitor (specially constructed for Toscanini) would captivate Bob's attention. I flashed a faltering smile when Wayne Newton sang "I Hate Myself For Loving You" for an audience of Bob Costa doppelgangers who adjusted their cuff-links with fervent heart-felt detachment. But *my* Bob appeared unabated; whistling, I turned in terror from the monitor's tier of bulging, caffeinated eyes. Into my hydrocephalic skull crept the concept of an infomation line for Bob. It might consist of an hour-long ad for tunnel detergent; or a demo of a pipe-cleaner recycler, in which an ersatz blonde crooned to moist Arabs—massaging hemeralopic egos as she rinsed their stems of scum.

Holed in a holding pattern of hours, when I feared I might never again watch the sun's glimmer detensify against the lubricious ripplings of Mariah Carey's lower lip, my focus naturally swivelled to schemes for seedy seduction. *I'm far too harmless to be labelled sexist,* I realized; imitation being my singular skill, I resolved, in my dying hours, to exercise it ruthlessly on the rich and faithless. *Norse goddesses and game show pointers beware,* I shrieked; *peeled Venuses in seal-furs will pale to Swedes before my potent impersonations.* First, I'll render my best Don Kirschner imitation over candlelight; then proffer a heap of memorabilia, signed and glazed in a fine Bernaise casement. Finally, I'll mime my greatest pasquinade: a quodlibet on the left-hand arpeggiations of Art Tatum, a snuffed pianist who once had original ideas. *Sure, sure, that'll work,* I purred. *Prestidigitations sho' nuff wow them pulchritudinous whelps.* Raptly, I recalled how patrons had thrilled to my counterfeit compositions at the Augustan Society last March, when I'd executed a waffle company jingle designed to air between segments of a Hanna Barbara cartoon based on The Death Of Julius Caesar: "Ego Ergo Eggo."

Suddenly, the number eleven button lit on the car-startion panel. Jostling us with cocktail-shaker verve, the elevator ascended; when the door lurched open like a Parkinsonian eye, my snake and I were freed. In the scalding glare of hallway florescence, Bob went light-headed and tried to embrace a syringe holder; but it was I and not my snake who slipped most drastically on freedom's peelings.

As my SWAT team of backup singers revived me by the Moorish wall, I lay awake for long and arduous hours, mentally tuning my array of pitched Palmetto Bugs. And it was there, held slightly aloft on a rhombus of hired Ronettes, that I suddenly realized my folly: despite earlier fears, it now seemed doubtful that Bob had represented my signal danger in Toscanini's lift. Rather, my chances leapt and panted on the sandy floor of the cracked terrarium beneath the monitor.

Never underestimate the amphibian, I told myself in the midst of mortal shock. *The most poisonous land animal is, as you know, the frog.* Overcome, I flattened and thinned to the page you are holding now.

To the former semi-celebrity turned fictive, life becomes a hypothetical attention span advancing retinally to the edge of a plank bleached calcium white. Yet even here, subsisting on the energy of the reader's interest, there is one beneficial effect. My sole and signal consolation is this: no former pirate, marooned on a page and conscripted to live as ink, has trouble communicating. I find no difficulty in making my last wants known.

Carry me, girls, to the bin where bandleader's wands lie broken. Handle me gingerly before I'm faxed to the home office. And please make sure that when I'm crumpled and tossed, Will Lee triggers a sample of shattering glass.

Technophilia's Last Wave

> The bottom of the sea is cruel.
> —Hart Crane, "Voyages"

That irksome itch caused by unwanted commercial grafts—synapse and cache, ego and prosthesis—is now nearly abated. Craning between levels of rhetoric, today's chin doctor proves unable to splice one text to the next. Language blurs under anesthesia, ruining our latest array of Nintendo quest sagas that pass for writing programs. Cosmetic surgery's luster dies like neon's glimmer reflected in stripes on a chrome skateboard swerving into the Holland Tunnel. As Future Fetishism™ dims to a pansemantic state of immersion, technophilia's focus remains unreal: a centaur's engine of dimwit's hide and dickhead's chthonic will.

•Syntax•

Fuck cyberpunk. That was the language of Nerdic interface, not fusion. A prosthetic limb is the driftwood of the expanded body. If we cannot permanently freeze our *selves* into fragments, then we must recognize our *language* to be engaged in a multi-directional syntax. It is all the same synthetic flesh, so Koreshian mock-revelations schismatize when the membrane splits and the wound cascades with blood.

141

•Utopias•

Ultimately, technophilia is only one facet of exolinguistics. Virtual Passivity (spiritual materialism) might be attractive to cultists—the computer-image-as-astral-body trope will doubtless appeal to the credulous skeptics of any pseudo-Christian society. But when we tire of floating in man-made, defective heavens; when we weary of predicting new ascendencies in the HD-partitioned pantheon of prophets, we return to the evidence of our unimportance: the sea.

•The Convict Stripped•

The late nineties will initiate the destruction of the narcissist's temple: the unspoken tenet that our culture is somehow more worthy than that of the unenlightened. Even anticrowds that fragment into uni-racial, sex-differentiated cliques will discover they are simply exchanging one kind of narcissism for another. Survivors of the (n)Euromantic eighties—who once flaunted futurist jewelry and the impossible costumes of economic automatism—will acquaint themselves with the texture of global nakedness.

•Lenses•

Pseudo-adventurers belong to the tides. Innovation is not a matter of fetishizing computers, *nor even of reacting against them*. The Mac is now a part of what we see—a metonymic subset, like Vermeer's camera obscura, or Chuck Close's photographic canvas. *Virtual* is an aspect not of *reality* but of *representation*: the *desktop* is merely a module for *transposition*.

Only a fool would condemn the computer's place in society. Fiction foregrounds the implications of change: the writer is no more at fault for technofetishism than a weapon can be blamed for murder. Since SF is a kind of techhead magic realism, Gibson's stylistic gift was to make the tool and user *appear* to fuse. Yet it was precisely because Gibson *didn't* understand computers that *Neuromancer's* fictitious future rang true for a decade of novices.

We now know far too much to believe in centaurs. Case's cranial jack is a dream-wet saline implant, the prosthetic metaphor of an oneiromantic surgeon.

•Tilted Aquarium•

The informed response to advances in automation is not to become half machine but to recognize that automation functions as a bridge in the collective body. The nerd who identifies with hardware is as deluded as the surgically-modified stripper who confuses autofetishism for confidence. Enhanced or undiluted, perceptions recombine when we stop the process of fragmentation in ourselves. If something happens to me when I turn on my computer, or when I kill a man, then I am adjusting my balance to suit the slightest circumstance—a flashing hotel sign, for instance, or the physique of a lover who triggers my random conditioning.

With awareness comes the *modus* of immersion: it is interesting to feel neither separate nor linked. To trace the collective pronoun *we* to the singular *I* until synaptic etymology proves that *I* is irrefutably unalone.

•Ethics Are Irrelevant•

I do not disbelieve in oxymorons like *personal morality*, but I cannot seriously pretend I am either good or bad. I veer closer to the nerve when my tendencies are not reformatted into antonyms—which is why I believe in scrutinizing all cognizant impulses until clarity fuses their fragmented program like the flame of a welding tool.

•Uxoromancer•

With the sweep of the tide, the corpse is pulled into the water. As present culture dissolves into history, so one cadaver deliquesces into the next. There is nothing terrible in this. Since civilization is the signature of a static, beachbound god, it should trouble no one that a certain divine signature is always Johnathan Swiftly erased. Our country, our technology and our religion are mere prosthetics; deal with dementia's depths and the ocean awaits. *If you can fuse these elements*, sea's gnosis says, *your death will be endless, your life resolute; the lost droplets of your personality will merge to a lasting self; and your treasured terminal will sign off automatically.*

An Inquiry Into Subjective Evolution

Confessions From A Glass Booth On A Traffic Island In Times Square

For many years, I believed that if mankind's worst fate were possible, then religion had lost its power to console. It seemed futile to sheathe such a vicious reality in vacant delusions. Others might have pretended to intuit the purpose of life and the provenance of the soul, but I lacked such comforts. Since I could detect no higher purpose beyond the biological imperative, nor verify the durability of the spirit after the deterioration of the mind, I concluded that a realistic understanding of life required a stringent rejection of hypothetical absolutes. Excluding the possibility of immortality from what could be proved, I replaced mystical beliefs with nihilism. God and Heaven were traded for death under a pallid sky.

The limitations of existence had not always seemed so claustrophobic. As an adolescent, I had experienced strange moments of bliss that I later tried to describe to my intellectual friends. These descriptions were pronounced inscrutable and vague. Discouraged by my peers, demoralized by the divorce of my parents and by the death of my first lover, I turned from the raptures of Blake and Antoine de Saint-Exupery to the fatalism of Poe and Baudelaire. *Les Fleurs Du Mal* was virtually to become my bible.

Though Baudelaire was superficially a Christian, he seemed to explain The Infinite as Death's leer; as a kind of inescapable bondage. Morality was a cowardly, hypocritical retreat from damnation. My condition was irredeemably wretched; my brief purpose was "to produce some noble verse" in order "to show that I am not lower than those whom I despise."

I now know that Baudelaire's temperament is not so easily distilled. But at the time, he seemed to exemplify the nobility of skepticism. Cravenly, I aped his smile of scorn. However mawkish and flawed they might seem today, my early verses railed at the imbecility of nothingness.

For me, Poe was to exemplify the innocence of corruption. His sonnet to his wife's mother, his "Ulalume" and "Annabel Lee," seemed to voice my maudlin disillusionment. His litanies entranced me to spells of deluded bombast—and I had reason to be easily beguiled.

At thirteen, I'd seduced a girl in a theater, then bragged about it so shamefully that I couldn't even say hello to her without feeling horrible—let alone accept the reality of my own selfishness. So I invented elegies detailing an imaginary car accident in which she died, and conjured scenarios in which I passed the wreckage of the crash each day en route to school. At fourteen, I slashed my wrists over a twenty-one-year-old lover whose faithlessness seemed to afford me a reason for self-sacrifice. And all throughout those years, I wrote poems and songs to the first girl, Carol, whom I'd mentally put to death, promising devotion in neo-Edwardian prosody. On some level, I was voicing my shame at having betrayed my mother. But on another, Romance was my refutation of the afterlife. In matters of love, sacrifice meant self-negation. That seemed to comprise humankind's only shot at nobility.

I remained oblivious to the pitfalls of this position for several years. But my preoccupation dissolved when I enrolled at Marylhurst College at seventeen. The disembodied presence of nuns for teachers, the admonitions of my father, the assertions by my twenty-six-year-old girlfriend that my mere existence caused her physical and emotional pain—all conspired to distill my death-wish through art. *If the worst is true, then let me believe the worst.* Nightly, I listened to recordings of Gustav Mahler, Gesualdo, Schumann, Hugo Wolf, Alban Berg; and studied the casualties of literature: Ernest Dowson, Christina Rosetti, Paul Verlaine, Jules Laforgue, Sade, Bataille, Nerval, John Keats, John Clare, Virginia Woolf, Lautreamont, Thomas Lovell Beddoes, Hart Crane and Robert Lowell. It seemed my task was to memorize art's sweep of self-negation in order to martyr myself. Dutifully, I studied medieval and post-romantic music—those monoliths to the elegance of earlier deaths.

After months of unrest, I stopped sleeping for weeks. Frustrate ambitions worried me until dawn. I constantly fretted that I was hurting my girlfriend by living. My father felt I had failed him by majoring in music. At the same time, it seemed that in attaining manhood, I had deserted my mother. Loving her, I wished for my masculinity to drain away.

After sleepless weeks—weeks in which the shreds of sleep worsened to eidetic bile—madness came to replace my waking world with nightmare. Standing before the mirror in my mother's bathroom, I watched my reflection become ghosted by another. Mother's face grew vivid and luminous, obscuring my own. Her orange-red lipstick caught the sunlight, glowing like melted crayon as my smile curved into hers. The sunlight swelled in that lavender bathroom invaded by lilacs.

Assuaging my selfhood, I fled—only to return when I heard a fly dash itself against reflective walls. Opening the door, I felt the suffering of the fly: it careered through the bathroom, an unevolved soul in pain. In its restlessness, I caught the glint of an immortal enmeshed in a ball of barbed shit. I endured its agonies; I wept for its desperation. I could do so little, I thought, for an unconscious mote of soul-life. Yet I knew that the fly was evolving. I opened the window and let it out. I wanted the thing I'd rescued from pain to heal.

I found my cat in the next room and petted her, sneezing all the time because of my allergies. Through her purring, she seemed to exude the torment I'd caused her as a child. Now that no one else petted her, I felt her loneliness. I resolved to pet her with tissues from that day on. But for those immediate hours, she had need of my hands. Touching her, I felt the pain of her surgical sexual disfigurement (spayed). She had so far to evolve, and I had not helped until now.

Weeks later, my madness worsened. I watched my body perform acts while I observed it. My feet marched stupidly from kitchen to bathroom; hands robotically threw cheese into the toilet. I could not stop my body, especially when walking.

One day, I sleepwalked into the abyss. It happened so innocuously—my hand was cutting bread while I watched dully: *slice*-bread/*slice*-bread/*slice*-bread/*slice*-the-bread-had-ended-and-there-was-my-arm: (blade) *S* (poised) *L* (to) *I* (cut) *C* (the) *E* (skin) ...*STOP*. My right hand caught my left wrist just before the blade sank into my arm. Distantly, I heard a rising howl. I closed my eyes, and in my imagination, looked down.

I literally stood at the edge of a cliff—yellow dust trickled bottomward from my bootheel—with incurable madness shrieking beyond the edge.

I grabbed the phone and called my friend, Mary Miller. She was still at work and mentioned something about needing to work overtime. Nevertheless, hearing my voice, she took the day off and rushed to her apartment to meet me. Frantically, I called a cab. The dispatcher said there were none. I raised my voice and she heard the howl of the cliff. A cab, she said shakily, was already on its way.

I counted the measures of imaginary overtures until the cab arrived. The driver held open the door. After I got in, I gripped the handrests until my fingers hurt. Each red light, each traffic snarl, contorted my scowl to a tighter rictus grimace. Attempting to calm me, the driver made tactless jokes. "A guy could go *nuts* in this traffic," he said with a worried laugh. Then he swore at the driver in front of us: "C'mon, lady, *c'mon!*..."

Finally, he let me off at Mary's. She buzzed me in; I ran up the steps and into her room. She asked me how I felt and I told her everything: The madness flooded out of me in weighted tones. Fluidly, I confessed my fear of losing my masculinity; of either trying to be gay and failing my father, or of being straight and hurting my mother; of being too dominant and somehow killing my girlfriend. "I can't look at you," I told her in a voice pitched four stories down. "I can't look at you because you're too beautiful." And I *couldn't*: because I wanted to fuck her, to fuck my beautiful angel. Instead, I listed everything I'd ever feared; every flaw in my character, every adultery in my short, faithless life; I described my sadistic dreams and wretched fears. I confessed to every crime I imagined I'd committed. *I couldn't look her*—then finally, I did. She was weeping uncontrollably, though my eyes were passive, dry.

And still I kept confessing my crimes: against Carol, Jamie and Jill, the three girls I'd loved; against Jim and Peter, two boys I'd teased in grade school because their friendship was "special"; for the time I'd failed my nephew by not protecting him from bullies; for the greatness I'd never attain; for the times I'd betrayed myself by acting conventional. I told her every lie I'd ever invented; I told her of every frog, every insect I'd ever tortured. Slowly, my voice rose in tone as Mary wept.

When my pitch reached some weightless tessitura, I finally heard it: My own voice penetrated a crowd of impersonations. It cut through the voices of those whom society and my father expected me to be. It ascended like the violin in the "Sanctus" of Beethoven's *Missa Solemnis;* like the pure tone of a fourth position high E piercing through a clouds of choral counterpoint; like a lone angel soaring past Michelangelo's wingéd wars.

At the very instant when I first heard my own voice, something swept through me that seemed to involve the entire universe: I *felt* the breadth of spiritual evolution. I saw a vision: of matter, located in hydrospace, in the act of becoming gas and bubbling to the ocean's surface. Matter represented the sleeping soul, which became weightless before it floated through a sea of unrest. When it rose past the water, it merged with air.

Heaven swept through me for decades or hours. Then my madness returned, and I fell back into my body's barbed crib. Fluctuating between states, I stayed with Mary for days. I was still too airy; not grounded; a box without a bottom.

By the time I returned home, I was resolute but considerably saner. Soberly, I looked through religious and philosophical texts—for anything which corroborated the image of hydrospace. Eventually, I found reference to my vision in the Upanishads, and in the *Srimad Bhagavatam*: these texts explained levels of spiritual evolution as the *three gunas*: Tamas (matter), Rajah (water) and Sattwa (air). Tamas was inertia; Rajah, restlessness; and Sattwa, purity. Eventually, one had to become free even of Sattwa, the highest guna, the Vedanta said.

For months, I read St. John of the Cross, Meister Eckhart, *The Perennial Philosophy*, Kabir, Blake, Rilke, St. Theresa, St. Seraphim of Sarov, "The Graces of Interior Prayer," St. Francis, the *Gita* in several non-airport translations, *The Cloud of Unknowing*, *The Method of the Siddhas*, *The Book of the Tao*, Suzuki's texts on Zen, Kirpal Singh's *Yoga of Celestial Sound*, Ramana Maharshi, the Cabala, the Torah, Yeats's *A Vision*. I pored over everything I could find to interpret my experience.

Transformation involved commitment: sadly, I was forced to break from my friends for a year and read in seclusion. I continued working on music with my teachers, who, understandably, wanted to hear nothing of my revelations. I saved those for an old, inspired sister in the nun's infirmary—a woman with Parkinson's disease who taught me certain secrets of the Russian Orthodox Church.

As my initial certainties faded, months lengthened to seasons of study. Soon, I was able to remember my past with purposeful clarity. As a child, I had walked on railroad tracks in the sunlight, feeling no separation between my brain and the sun, no helmet of bone to separate thought from light. It was as if my head had been an open bowl and my higher mind floated billions of miles above me—sending pleasure and illumination into the decillion skulls of the world.

To me, *The Little Prince* by Exupery and the paintings of Giotto had represented a tiny place invaded by a presence. That place was the sensual world. The invader was the sun. I'd felt that nakedly as a child and had merely grown sick from years of intellectual denial.

To this day, I can't be certain those moments were true or delusive. At my maddest, I was convinced I could hear people's thoughts. Waiting at the bus-stop, I once felt my presence overlap with that of an elderly lady. I was sure I felt the unrest and disappointment in her mind; I said some coded word to her in a kind voice; I felt her heart unknot. Many times in that period, I experienced similar moments—moments in which I said careful things to put people at ease. Perhaps these people heard something more innocuous than my meaning, or merely humored me with prosaic smiles. I can't say, anymore than I can be sure what happened when I tried to caress the torture out of my cat. Nor what occurred when I felt the suffering of the fly; the ball of barbed shit running into walls; the feces-thing that blindly tried to rise.

If I learned my purpose from spiritual books, I found the difference between the velocity of *personal* and *collective* evolution in science. Studying a flea through a microscope, I read its morphology: its very anatomy seemed designed to fuck up other beings. Its pincers that grabbed, its sucking mouth parts, its armor, its skull—a helmet of hatred—all were made to infect and destroy other species. Over time, I realized that the flea is like society. One can identify with society and wait for the societal flea to evolve into something higher, but that kind of evolution only happens over eons. I decided it was better not to wait; that it was better to evolve beyond society and initiate change.

I can't pretend that what transpired in madness was literally true. I can only express what I felt during that tumultuous summer, and what I still trust enough to accept after all this time.

I believe that, just as a video screen is a low-res representation of the reality it monitors, so our senses reveal the merest fraction of the actual world. I believe that the presences of human beings are not separate from one another; that my perception of non-separation is verified each time I walk through a crowd. The image of isolate beings is projected as an allegorical overlay for *reference*—i.e., in a form which my limited sight can interpret usefully to navigate my body from here to there. But in another, prioperceptive sense, I feel I am floating among presences which blur at the edges. These presences bleed together like green lights in water—their diffuse haloes blending at the edges—so that their focal points are individual but not hermetic. In other words, we are simultaneously computers and convergent lights.

For lovers, even the *focus* is blurred by the act of penetration. I *know* I have touched the inside of a lover's head and spoken her thoughts, just as I know our spirits and beings were fused—immersed in prioperception's depths.

I believe that the movie screen of human eyesight shows its recipient a display of separate beings for *mere convenience*, but that voices entreat the viewer from behind the screen. The deeper presence of a crowd is liquid, infusing the screen's readout of puppets. The oversoul flows though sight to suggest the spirit world.

My first college course in philosophy yielded the term *empiricism.* After my time with Mary, I seized it and tried to apply it to my experience. Then as now, I remain a spiritual empiricist. I believe only in what I have tested.

The same holds true for this essay. As written *testimony*, my experience proves nothing. Do my certainties corroborate your own, *mon semblance*? How can anyone know unless they, too, have seen the angels? My memories cannot be interpreted as *evidence*. None of you has ever lived in this body.

Progress is hermetic, the traveler's life visible only as paradox. Transformations of the self take place in a glass booth, where each surge of pedestrians presses against the soul's transparent walls.

But the walls are only a convention. Language has a pseudo-facade: the black beetle-armor of typeface which conceals the ether of thought. Somehow, the meaning slips through, misting all outsiders.

That mist is enough to carry me to the end of this sentence. For the moment, I am rapt in my glass booth, confessing my prioperception on a traffic island in Times Square. But I am no specimen in a Petri dish, no schizogen-drunk dog swaying to inscrutable music. My breath frosts the glass; heat rises from my throat like a snake made of vapor. It curves through the white skin of this page to lick your eyes.

Fig VI. *When Sleep Comes Down*

When Sleep Comes Down

To Mary Beth, whatever she is: alive, dead or dreaming.

What he was attracted to was being with a person sexually when they
were not conscious.

—Dr. Judith Becker, on her interview with Jeffrey Dahmer

When the telephone rang at four A.M., in a loft cluttered
with scores and music notebooks—notebooks seared and
starred with expressive markings like seismographs of
restrained psychosis—Gizmo hadn't been sleeping. He'd
been jerking off slow motion to the voice he heard now:
the voice on the receiver, a sample from his wettest nightmare. That drawl in a sandpaper rasp belonged to Jill—the
girl he'd been picturing off and on for seventeen hours. He
tried to make her say where she was, but she kept changing the details. "In a bar," "with some friends," "on the corner"—whatever the location, the exchange that was probably taking place made his eyes crinkle. She was broke,
straight and shivering. To take care of her problem, the
mode of commerce was sex for D.

He put on his camouflage raincoat and booked. Outside,
the rain had just let up, and the sidewalks of Alphabet Town
were as slimy as the skin of a queen termite. He checked all
the streets in his neighborhood, then the abandoned buildings. He pretended he wasn't looking for her, just to free his

155

peripheral vision. But it was when he'd really given up—not told himself he had—that he found her at last.

He pulled her out of a rusted Plymouth by a fistful of hair so close to the scalp that at first it felt unrecognizable. But the blonde ponytail he'd tugged compulsively for nine months had been abbreviated to match some trick's twist. As he dragged her through the empty windowframe, the first thing he saw was a Tenaxed flat-top dyed auburn. Her face came into the light without a wince of discomfort—her tanned complexion ravaged by skin popping, her eyes one-sided, like limo glass.

But her figure had grown so vivid in his imagination that he didn't have to decipher the darkness to replay a slow pan: high breasts, a torso like an hourglass thickened, an ass so full that when he spanked her, it quivered, the brown cheeks darkening to a deep rose. Even like this—fucked unconscious—she was fine enough to have ridden in a rich trick's Lincoln until he left her there, used and useless.

When she was half-way out of the car, an empty bottle of Hycotuss expectorant slid across her chest: prescription codeine. She'd probably raided some college girl's medicine cabinet and spent the night here because she hated the rain as much as she feared her own intelligence.

He spread open her corduroy jacket. Slow motion roaches crawled out of the pocket: a sugar donut fell out, half-eaten. She was feeding the bugs again, as narcotics ate away the fist between her ribs.

She'd written a message on her wrist in red ink: **Princess of Morticians**. That's what she'd called herself on the phone, her English lit. mind remembering Thomas Lovell Beddoes as her body leaned against the booth, performing acts. She'd called just to know she had an out, a faraway squeeze in the granite world, because he was the boyfriend whom junky girls picture when they dream of kicking. (They don't need to clean up—yet—they just want to keep him on file.)

She was a sick twist, which was why he dragged her into a cab and home to his mattress. She was nearly a toss-up, but that didn't matter: he was drawn to her death-trance eyes, to her olive skin, to those cheek-bones so high and chiseled they were like Hepburn in plaster of Paris, a statue poised too close to the window, so that soot and rain had changed the smooth texture into something the blind could read.

As soon as he'd dropped her onto his bed, he pulled off her jeans. She wasn't wearing panties. He touched her pussy and it was wet. He sniffed his fingers, but they smelled more like a dream of excitement than a procession of tricks.

"I'm always tracking you down and you always look worse than you did the night before."

"Huh?...Giz...I feel like...what are you doing..."

They were naked now and he was fucking her awake. "I've been saying your name, Jill. I licked you some, but you were already wet. I thought you could hear me."

"No, but....it's okay....just let me go to the bathroom."

When she staggered back to him, he set her down gently and slid it in. He fucked her until the haze faded from her eyes, and she was holding onto him like the last girder of sanity's bridge.

"....it hurts, Giz....fuck me harder..."

He imagined he was fucking her in the alley with the rats and the piss-smell and the shattered glass. He imagined dying with her, walking her through the graveyard until she could do it herself, sort of, tromping stiffly down the darkening path in soiled white lace, a firefly crawling up her arm. Until they were all the way into the woods, branch-shadows closing on her singed whiteness, the gray sky massing to black. As if night were crawling over her, a cluster of spiders.

His come was dust in a bone-saw paradise. When he finally looked down, he saw *nothing*. Her body grinned up at him, her bone structure the mirror of a rictus smile.

They lay there for hours, warm and distracted. Jill didn't offer to clean up because that kind of promise involved the future, and Giz knew she didn't have one. So when she excused herself to go to the bathroom, he was half-aware. He didn't pay much attention when she took her crumpled coat with her.

When sleep came down, he thought absently about a song he was writing for a new act, an industrial artist signed by the alternative department at Effector. He lay there trying to be patient long after the inspiration had faded. When he finally knocked on the bathroom door, nearly an hour had passed. She was probably shooting up in there. That was like her—to lean behind bathroom doors, hating herself until the rush came and she hated no one. *I should have checked her pockets for works,* he thought as he opened the door.

Her corpse was keeled over beside the fixture's porcelain base, one arm still braced against her stomach. Her eyes were wide and pinned. Her muscled body was beautiful even in agony, and now it was empty. The emblem of a dead soul.

He carried her outside and dumped her in an abandoned building. He had to, he told himself—it was either that or get nailed for possession. Record execs referred to drug abuse as a "health problem," but even with studio clients, *addict* was the wrong rep to have. Sentimentality is a bad substitute for respect.

For days, he walked around stricken, imagining her voice, her breasts dangling over him, her eyes encrypted. When he thought of her, he wept, telling himself he loved her. But what he really loved was death. She was marked for it as surely as track marks had burned decay's history into her arm. He himself didn't do drugs. He wanted death's embrace vicariously, to feel the arms close over him while he was fully conscious, feeling the come shoot out of him like an arpeggio.

158

Each night at dusk, at four A.M., when he remembered her, his purple thoughts acquired a black sheen. Buried by strangers, forgotten by friends, it seemed that her image was being replayed in his mind alone. Recalling her last night on earth made him feel like Dowson inside, an Edwardian drinking himself to death in pain and shame. Or staggering down brick inroads, a mongrel clipped by hooves. Transfixed by the carriage lantern as the night-wood wheeled to blackness.

Orchestrations

(i.i) Title Page HTML

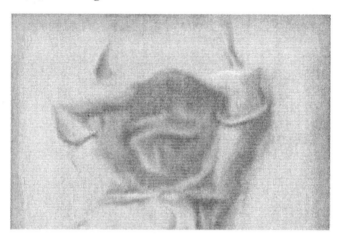

Paralyzed Paradise/Matterland

©1993, (S)crypt Carnographies, Ltd.

(Ideally, consecutive words should materialize on the screen *letter by letter*, accreting into sentences and paragraphs until the selected space reaches its phrased or punctuated close. At that time, the text should vanish and all words in boldface (that serve as keyed links) remain, glimmering like Cheshire grins until the reader selects a single lingering keyword. Such a script would be preferable to this one, because people whose synapses are shaped by video games find normal story-space scripting *static*.)

•Please Select Either: (1.a)**Paralyzed Paradise**; or (1.b)**Matterland**.•

(1.a) Blighted Bodies

He couldn't find her anywhere. Wearily, Giz/Ren sprinted through studios A to D; gaze-panned the lounge;
returned to scrutinize the vox/orgy niche behind A's
glass booth doors before peregrinating from the stairwell to the downstairs hall. After looking outside the
elevator, he gave up. When Rachael vanished, only Jared
(2.a)**remained**: a ferrule face, its withheld emotion a
vanishing perspective of patterns. Outside, the street
felt like a hospital seeded with seminal skulls: from an
adjacent rooftop, IV bottles crashed into gutters, collid-
ed along chicken wire patch bays of streetlight and telephone pole, streaming coagulants in fat black strands. It
was over for the night. Liz had (2.b)**emptied** his interest and no one, not even the techs, could feel its fluo-
rescence.

(1.b) Sutured Souls

TANGLEWOOD PHARMACY

the sign's faint neon read. Just below it, the legend

Drugs • Paints • Oils • Toiletries

raked the corner of D and 5th Street with exsanguine
light—its halo extending to the far side of the projects. This was the only storefront junkies didn't
crowd, since the pale proprietor refused to sell rubbing alcohol or baking soda to a skank. Many times,
Giz had followed the sign's radiance on queasy walks
down D at five a.m. With the streetlamps browned to
glove-compartment dim, he watched for the place
like some checkpoint between fear and wired aware-

163

ness. Finding the white glare helped to blur the creep of sidewalk steam; still, inches of mist (or must) swirled close to the street—a whorl of ashtray smoke that rose like anger. But he'd never seen a person walk through smoke without a sharpness at the edges. Now he noticed a figure shrouded in smog, a stratocumulus on legs—indistinct before turning the corner and floating into shadow. All he'd hoped for registered (2.b)**empty**, while all he'd hated held up to wear him down. (And only this trace of paradise (2.c)**remained**.)

(2.a) Glacier

By the bronze light of the
tube-tray behind Liz's amp,
substrata of rot and romance
etiolated to ice-floe. This was
it—Giz had only a dead girl
to embrace, the inflatable
saint of a jack-off's missed
cliff remission. Trying hard
not to piss his black denims,
he knelt on dust-streaked
knees, slipped his hand past
the circuitry of the Marshall,
and squeezed: GLASS GNASH/
POCKETY-POCK/AN EXPLO-
SION FISTED IN
BLACK/•/SPILLED SOUL;
LOW FLAME/AN ACROBAT'S
SMOKING FRAME.

His oppressor was over. Liz paled, (5.)**nerve
terminals trailed...**

(2.b) ....

He tried to search his pockets, only to find his hands
themselves missing. Attempts to wriggle his fingers
burned vertigo-inducing transmitters from neuron to
receptor to target neuron: synapses leading from
brain to extraneous brain. Wincing, he receded into
his head but found no focus. He endured the sight of
his mind through Liz's eyes, then felt her flinch when
sensing his recoil. Singed genitals ignited like parallel
trashcans, dual diamonds on the same playing card
deuce, the deck flung into an even larger fire. Their
feedback peaked until he looked away. As he
boomeranged away from Liz, the act of turning
inward flattened him to a headless mass. He coruscat-
ed in fog, connected to far too much—a spirit in soft-
ware searching for flesh-fixed ports.

*...wait...what has happened to us...where is this
place...and why is she doing this...*

Seven ellipses cleared to avenues, then dead ends. All
led to the alley of transmigration. Synapse-forced fingers writhed involuntarily. Locked in his body, he
watched night whiten to mid-day, street change locus,
the copper-wire soul he loved objectify (3.)**herself**.

(2.c) Tiers

Ruefully, Giz/Ren overtook the logo in old-time neon,
its bloodless pink light glimmering under a plastic
guard. He turned the corner and hit a blackout of
sable space—until penumbras shifted into gradients
of gray. The figure still glinted directly in front of him,

walking through abysses with a swish of the backside. Sadly, he remembered that familiar, feminine
sway. He overtook the figure, leaned closer—and
touched a knot of copper. The figure stopped; neck
wrinkled; head turned back. The face, a Giacometti in
coat-hanger wire, belonged to Liz. The skeleton lived
in art, a death remembered. He stopped looking at
her because he was always looking. Tentative steam
on the sidewalk darkened to strands; must pellicles
re-gathered, sparked. Trashed gravel spumed to
corneal censer, brightening sudden graffiti: Doré etchings in phosphorescent paint, a blueprint of the heav-
en he'd dreamed about, where Liz the ghost could
never bolt or use. "Mad Dog," dead dealers cooed from
empty ledges. "Last chance for Mad Dog. Nightmare.
Skeleton." Wire whitened to ligature, whispers choired
antiphonal winds. The air itself massed Liz/Giz's
(5.)**opened souls** merging.

(3.) Exhumed Through Sewage

Newly minted and scoping the breadth of Potter's
field, transmuted eyes retrieved her sleep. A rectangu-
lar patch of rough dirt flickered red; the air surrounding it smelled of burning rubber—the psychic reek of
murder:—*her body lay under dirt at the range's center*. Frantically, Giz dropped to the ground and dug
with flattened hands; moments later, his fingertips
touched oxygenated bone. Fragile lines of soiled
white calcium emerged through dirt. Skeletal hands,
once lush and whorled, dissolved to a powder that
leaked into Giz/Ren's dreams. Distinctly, the powder
rose like a soul in wind—a kinetic haze—that floated
into the street, where dust transmogrified to corpse.
Asleep, Liz lay, OD'd, over (4.b)**grates of rain**.
Transversely, Possibility flowed Death's text into

166

loaded circuits:—I FUCKED HER OVER/I FAILED TO
HELP HER OUT:—

(4.a)FUCKED HER
(4.c)SAVED HER

*—like a lonely criminal's corpse leading live souls
downward.*

(4.a) Fucked Her Over

Yeah, I'm the one who was supposed to drag her
back into life. I thought it wouldn't matter that much,
you know, if she, like, failed to follow me home. So I
didn't sweat it, then. I denied how I felt. But all that's
over at this point. Cause I don't fucking care about
myself now that she's not around.

Drawn to sickness, I made her die. I parsed her
prayers like objections to foreplay and fucking. She
nicknamed me Thanatos because I'm the prissiest
shit: I feign compassion in order to slime the
wretched. My romantic/spiritual tastes incline toward
corpses. Now my beautiful bitch is dead and there's
only one place for me:

to die, fingers locked around a lit tube and pressing,
inhaling the voltage till I'm fused to the back of her
(2.a)**amp.**

(4.b) An Eye

Her socket/this pupil: the lens's wreckage dimmed
from see-through to oblique. Below that hole
stretched another lipless grin—a space surrounded
by maize, Indian corn, the teeth of a saint who

167

starved herself for psychosexual knowledge.
Unpenetrated by light, the pupil burned to ash in
ebony fire. Smoke-webs drifted into Giz's face; crumpled, fistic, the lens/film glowed autonomously, a tran-
sitive verb now modified by (4.b.i)**nothing**.

On hands and belly beside the grate, Giz
whispered/thought: *All martyrs are hedonists. They
slacken to vassals beneath the weight of day.
Licorice veins, rerouted down, involve the victim's
name, a mane. Skies park nowhere. Softened by
time, eyelets fill with ripening centipedes. Islets
frame such sunsets: blue beauty's orange erosion.*

Negative capability drove him headlong into sewage.
Leaning past the grate, Giz became that place.

(4.b.i) Grate

shadowy place extends from the hole like a
blister/pus-dream diced like an eye by the bars of the
grate/eye, bug-lash, trash in vivid windows/Giz prays
to Dead God he can keep holding onto that iron
visor/a clay finger pointing downward to traffic/so
far, so slow from here, that molded soot-chunks fall
like mascara'd asterisks from the sockets of statues in
some sky/lost in the cave of an idol's eyeless gaze/till
a black car slams his face into sudden
pavement/posthumous thoughts of Liz's lasting lash-
es/of lifelines extending to highways that vanish
between red hills capped in black/of an emptied
space for love turned gorgeous (5.)**grave**.

Giz lifted the grate and climbed inside a tunnel.
Drowning in sewage, the light in his body left.

(4.c) Saved Her

I traced her to a splintering floor in a wound-fucking
culthouse: lying in shadow on gray planks, face
pressed against the platform of a bed where Crowley-
obsessed biker junkies kept a fat woman doped, slit-
ting her folds with knives as they did her to death. Liz
was fucked up, of course: *I'm okay. They won't hurt
me. I'm not fat, y'know.* I dragged her downstairs,
knowing I couldn't phone the cops about the other
lady. Calling the ninth precinct meant killing us all.

When Liz downplayed the problem, I told her she
needed to kick. But she couldn't commit: she agreed
to a plan, then aborted the following day. I told her to
go to a meeting: she claimed no friend would escort
her. She strayed into traffic; fixed Cobra where X'd
people slept. She crouched alleys away, turning pale
when the maze resurrected her promise; replaying
her death, she broke online in a telephone booth. I
shrugged and said, *go ahead.* She thought I was
fronting. I took a walk, waited in diners, tore up reckless letters, arranged to interrogate the men I'd met in
the dark. I went back, lost it and told her I loved her.
Nobody listened. Lids and fist clenched permanently—unprimed for that final shock.

So the wound-fucking cult on C was the last place I
saw her alive. Caving, I finally called the precinct:
Girl, I'll follow you down. I'll fucking (2.c)**join** *you
when I find the coachman's car.*

Rob Hardin

(5.) Judgment: Manipulation

> God is Math.
> —Sally Cato

Skies lightened to magenta. The haze petrified to a sheet of slate. A detailed queue and a pair of thrones zoomed to god-size from tiny bits of blood and graying liquid.

In a settlement for bums and evicted families, Giz/Liz stood in a queue. It led to an infant couple enthroned in a grimy tent, delivering sentences simultaneously, side by side. When (h)h(i)e(s)r turn came, they narrowed their eyes and smiled.

"You know the old saw," they intoned to Giz/Liz in unison. "If you obsess on form, which you did, then everything becomes your drug. Then you start to need denser forms more often, and then you're asleep. That's where you're headed now, my boy and girl. The way we see it, you guise have only two choices: to tweak on Avenue (6.a)**C** or nod on (6.b)**D**. Our judgment reflects the limitations of yours."

"Yeah, right." Giz/Liz made the choice and settled into that sphere.

(6.a) Selfish Pleasure

On Watson and Sixty-Third, at the center of
Englewood, Chicago, light poured densified souls
through glittering blood-beams like marionettes outlined in ever-reddening sequins. Stripped of their last
etheric vestiges, Giz/Liz stood at the threshold of a
mansion. Whistling, they walked inside. As soon as
they closed the door, a tall, naked man with a stitched
crack running visibly from widow's peak to mohawked
genitals stepped out of an angled hallway, gesturing
toward its thirty-six chloroform-drenched rooms. He
led them to a locked door that opened on a shaft
descending to the next lowest floor. Startled, they
gaped back at him; then, noticing how the halves of
his body belonged alternately to giant and dwarf, they
turned away abruptly. Their deflected eyes signaled
the end of his hesitation. With a wide sheet of iron, he
struck their skulls concurrently. He said: "I'll shear
your nerve-ends for pleasure and sell your bones to
God." They sank though the third floor to the second,
an untransomed panoply of thirty-five doors barely lit
by dimmed gas jets. He kicked them though a chute
and they dropped to the basement furnace, where
they landed on a pedestal sprayed by blazing fuel jets.
Nerve-shocked, Giz/Liz thought: *We're angels in the
form of spheres; joined souls, four-armed, four-
legged, roll into heaven. If matter is life's disease,
then Death is* (7.)**venom**.

Fisted in flame, their skulls shrank to charcoal for the
fifth and final time.

171

Rob Hardin

(6.b) Mall of Martyrs

Their minds fixed on spheres of self-sacrifice, Giz/Liz
materialized in Camden, New Jersey—the fourth
poorest city in America. Among houses that moldered
like stacks of cardboard—waterfrayed cardboard
pulled from the lids of defective washing machines—
they skimmed matrices of razed neighborhoods;
netherstreets connected by geographic jump-cuts to a
region outside of Thailand; a weed-strangled murder-
mall ungoverned by muscle or law. Abandoned by
police, Camden/Thailand offered two forms of
release: Prime Time or Nintendo. Like no prior drug,
nor previous medium, these artificial daydreams
stripped and co-opted the imaginations of the shave-
skulled saved—until even the sanctified suffered
infernal dreams.

Giz/Liz wandered through Camden for hours before
locating its negative charge. They entered a shack
with gentle-eyed stiles, imagining interiors crowded
with orphans. But the worst home in the city
appeared the tamest: Martyr house.

Giz/Liz fell through a chute in the floor to a pit filled
with quicklime, which instantly dissolved their bones
to dust. "No resurrection for *you*," Emcee Mudgett
quipped as he raised the lever which closed the pit.

On a molecular level, (7.)**erasures** followed...

(7.) Tamas

Sleep, (i.i)**matter**. Death's intersection plunges past
a range of Tanguy objects sheathed in mold and
maille. It cruises through holes in a tunnel of tighten-
ing zeroes, to the lard-pearled bodies that clot the rest
home floor, clogging the hides of bile-obstructed
machines; to the factory that builds itself, melts its
own iron flesh, and consumes the oil it sweats to use
for fuel. It slides into sewage, grinds delicate innards
to twists of brittle shrapnel, rams headlong through
closing subway doors to freeze low scenes, prolong-
ing screams until they stretch to spindling legs, which
describe monoliths of crystal and obsidian, overlooking the workings of an urban landscape's see-through
Etch-a-Sketch, rods grimed silver with gristle and mer-
cury, like a city you hold in your palm to read in
sleep. It skims the pages of junkyards, sandpaper-
tongues the genitals of engines, bellies through silt at
the base of a chrome pond thick with cold, slow bub-
bles caught in a pocket of lava-turned-grooved-gray fist.

Yeah, sleep forever, Tamas. Born murdered, you leaf
through storied crosses, traversing transverse scripts
and eating Death's iridescence. Unstitched, the
sutured story stings; dissected, layered corpses ring.

Goodbye, cruel matrix; ultrarationalist magic
squares; determinist acts of aleatoric faith. You super-
impose architectural forms over music, as cerebral as
thirteenth century motets. You make me fail by forcing me to live in structures; by consigning me to
bloodcells—acrostic centuries like Tennyson's elegies
etched on the tomb of Gray.

Barbed archaisms catch, gutwired to roots. When
you hang yours overhead, leave mine inside the
(3.)**mine**.

Diane Di Prima: Ms. 45

Off-White Screen. Crawl In Black: "The road is the universal tomb, not the image of my freedom."—René Daumal, *L'Evidence Absurde*

FADE IN. A West Village flat, conspicuously unfurnished, with white walls, a wooden floor painted gray, and an open window overlooking Hudson Street. A bare mattress on frame and springs rests against the far wall. Scotch-taped above the mattress, a print of a Monet redundancy in Saniflush blue dangles and flaps. Periodically, a breeze rattles the window-glass. The clarity of the sunlight, and the wind-swept appearance of objects and people in the room, suggest a warm, balmy afternoon at the end of spring. The bed sags slightly under the weight of its occupants. DI PRIMA, a plump, withdrawn twenty-one-year-old mute who boldly expresses shyness in the language of locked ankles and intertwined limbs, lies huddled next to IVAN, a lanky, working class Austrian expatriate of nineteen. FADE OUT.

DI PRIMA
(V.O.)
(Black Screen.) When I was seventeen and hungry, the whole world seemed too dead to hold my interest. Days passed before I knew I was even alive. By the time I met

NEAL CASSIDY, I had nothing to hope for but the attention I thought I'd never get.

DISSOLVE *to white.*

NEAL changed all that.

SERIES OF STILL SHOTS *showing an idyllic diner-booth meeting: DI PRIMA in front of her empty plate, charmed; CASSIDY, clowning with sandwich; waitress in bg. wearily scowling.*

Slick, drunk and reeking, NEAL found me dabbing my eyes at the Tiffany Diner. He told me I was Mary Magdalen. Suckered, I gave him my address.

LAST SHOT: *CASSIDY facing DI PRIMA with serious gaze, hands clasping her shoulders.* FADE OUT.

I prayed he'd visit me, or write, at least. He never did. Instead, his writer friends arrived much later that evening. Clearing the candle fumes, they came in twos.

WHITE CAPTION: Summer, 1951. FADE IN. *Wearing only a flowery nightgown, generic bra and corset, DI PRIMA sits on her mattress in dim candlelight. From the left speaker comes the* (O.S.) *sound of knocking, hoarse male shouts and stifled laughter. Holding her collar together with one hand, DI PRIMA runs to the door.*

DI PRIMA
(V.O.)
ALLEN and JACK were the ones who took my virginity.

Reluctantly, DI PRIMA opens the door. ALLEN GINSBERG and JACK KEROUAC stumble in.

I still remember the commotion in my bedroom. ALLEN's skull and belly gleamed in amber candlelight. JACK grinned handsomely as he lifted my dress to inspect my cherry.

MEDIUM SHOT *of KEROUAC ripping away a frozen DI PRIMA's dress. CLOSE-UP MONTAGE of brutal trespasses. Hands slip beneath the corset band. Knuckles arch. Tongues lick shadowy hollows and openings.*

They said they were going to fuck me, so I nervously undressed. Throughout that midnight orgy, I did everything I possibly could to please them.

CLOSE-UP *of DI PRIMA's tear-stained face sandwiched between JACK's distracted grimace (FRONT) and ALLEN's leer (BACK).*

In return, they taught me lessons about life. But since I'd come of age as a fifties chick, their most important rule pertained to sex.

CUT TO *shot of KEROUAC using a teacher's pointer to jab at a spread-eagled, bound DI PRIMA as GINSBERG displays various typewriters and syringes. The two men ramble unintelligibly in the bg.*

No matter how fat, stupid, or self-obsessed he is, the bohemian chick must always fuck her guest, JACK said. If you don't fuck your guest, that means you're just hung up.

CLOSE-UP *of DI PRIMA's eye, duct-taped open: trembling and wide.*

Since fucking everyone was cool according to JACK, and since those two guys were the first friends I ever had, I believed them. I couldn't very well go along with my parents, right? I didn't realize till later that JACK and ALLEN had *lied...*

FADE OUT *like a pause at the end of a stanza.*

The incident left me mute, but that didn't matter. I was on the inside. I was a beat chick. I knew the words.

WHITE CAPTION: 1955. FADE IN *on* ORIGINAL SHOT *of DI PRIMA and IVAN.*

DI PRIMA
(V.O.)
It's hard to believe the orgy happened here.

CUT TO *IVAN, with the edges of DI PRIMA's legs and hands within the frame.*

IVAN
(Lazily rolling his R's) Vass gut, eh? Vassn't it gut, leetle Müte? Vassn't my vish fulfillment epizode gut for-r-r you, too?

CLOSE-UP. DI PRIMA, expressionless but for a slight forced smile, wants to speak but can only grunt provocatively.

DI PRIMA
Uh...Uh...

IVAN
(Sprechstimme) How I *luff* my *lee*-tle *feef*-ties *möte!* Der-r-r *mötes,* dey give der *pest ploh* jobs...

DI PRIMA
(V.O.)
I'd serviced him three times already, as I had so many other pigs. It was all they ever wanted anyway. So I couldn't tell

him it sucked to suck him off. Let IVAN have all the pleasure for now, I thought. My turn would come later, when it was time for his *dissection*.

TRACK *IVAN's head turning widely, jaw relaxed, eyes clouded.*

DI PRIMA
(V.O.)
How I despised him—for his naive self-interest...

DI PRIMA'S POV of IVAN's rib-cage stretched by fun-house mirror.

...his gangly, greenish body...

INSERT *of undersea eels sliding across one another.* DIS-SOLVE *to* CLOSE-UP *of IVAN's lips.*

...his insufferable smile, his plumber's kiss...

REVERSE POV. FULL VIEW *of DI PRIMA nodding and grinning hollowly, her shoulders hunched, her knees folded, her legs drawn beneath her in the shape of an angular conch.*

DI PRIMA

Uh! Uh!

DI PRIMA
(V.O.)
All my disgust would be set down in a vehemence of gushing, logorrheic, Lawrentian rhetoric; in metanarrative so mercilessly sprawling it would destroy his confidence and subvert his memories of conquest. I looked forward to drowning his identity in prose like theft, a prose of cons.

But for now, the impulse to retaliate locked itself in my double-jointed replies.

A working class rapist—how mindless, I thought. To IVAN, my grunts seemed counterfeit praise: coined at his expense. MEDIUM GROUP SHOT. *IVAN tosses DI PRIMA a work shirt and she pulls it over her head.*

DI PRIMA
(V.O.)
...just ignore the stench, I thought...
TRACK. *IVAN leaves bedroom through kitchen hallway.* INSERT *of thirties cartoon urinal coughing.* CUT TO FULL VIEW *of bedroom. IVAN whistles* OFF-SCREEN *until he walks* INTO FRAME *with a plate of scrambled eggs.* CUT TO CLOSE-UP *of DI PRIMA's nauseated grimace and protruding tongue.*

IVAN
Hey, Möte! Vant zum breakfazt?

DI PRIMA
(Disgusted) Uh! Uh!

IVAN takes a bite, tries to kiss her with egg dripping from his lips. She waves him off, leaves.

IVAN
Möte go...to powder byootiful cheek, huh huh huh huh...

DI PRIMA walks INTO FRAME *in a beret and false goatee, pulls out a Colt revolver with a Wilson Suppresser and shoots IVAN. As he slides off the bed, too surprised even to feel betrayed, she stands there, penumbral in hall-light, her shadow flooding the recessed floor at her feet with blackness.*

IVAN

(Moaning) Vot der-r-r-r-r fock!!...how can you come...you ar-r-r-re friendly möte...

DI PRIMA
(V.O.)

(Facing the camera) Yeah, *I* was JACK KEROUAC's fuckin' fifties mute, huh? I was definitely the slut queen no-tell motel on *his* two-lane blacktop: a well-oiled wand-warmer like all the other skanks. Yup, *all* us bitches got fucked over in those days—knocked up, abandoned, raped in our sleep by drunken poets, overlooked, cheated on, discouraged (like Dorothy Wordsworth and Lady Montagu) from writing our own novels—we *really* only existed to keep house, breed, or volunteer for the slit research of NEAL Fucking CASSIDY. But all of that was about to change—permanently. When I finally found my own screwed-up voice, my music was murder to Charlie M. Parker's ears...

As IVAN moans, DI PRIMA pulls out a huge plastic book with a hollow center, opens it, lops off one of IVAN's hands, and throws it inside the book. Animated cartoon globules rises from his stump's spurting gore to the center of the frame, where they gather to form the ghastly red letters of the title:

DIANE DI PRIMA: MS. 55

dir. & wr. by Abel F. Cainan, low-key auteur
(Based on the unsubstantiated bragging
of DI PRIMA's cellmate, SUSAN ATKINS)

CLOSE-UP *of IVAN's face.*

IVAN

But—you are kill me? How can you come? You are female in feefties vorlt.

DI PRIMA
(V.O.)

Get over it. Centuries before the beats made a character flaw out of disciplined behavior, amazons conquered civilizations and women ruled. I've always known it intuitively, just as you grasp a woman's second-class status today. But I hadn't really understood the mindset of my homicidal ancestors until two years ago last Tuesday. The problem that solved it all was JACK, who had drenched my uterus in seed he'd promised to spill, leaving me with *his fetus*—a fetus for which JACK's delinquent head scoped zero responsibility. After nine months of indifferent recriminations, circumstances drove me to an act of murder: deserted by JACK, and too poor to enlist the aid of illegal doctors, I was forced to give *myself* a bloody abortion.

It all seemed so painful at first (my hand shook violently, my scalpel felt cold and biting, the hose leaked tiny body parts onto my gown) until I heard my sewage problem scream. I'd waited too long for the operation, and now JACK's...embryo...felt the pain acutely, a pain acutely expressed by his full-blown vocal cords. But when I murdered JACK's...child...I screamed more loudly than even it had screamed.

That's when I first heard my own voice, the invention of a cribbed death, a murderer's emergence. Soon, I knew, my voice would swallow larger victims. An aborted life marked the end of my killing silence.

IVAN
(Suddenly waking from the pain) But...you kent do ziss...If you are killer, dey vill say you are not real vooman...

DI PRIMA
(Aloud)
They won't say that—not ever. From now on, NEAL and JACK and ALLEN and the rest—that whole, interminable queue of braggarts and rapists—they'll know me as *MS. FIFTY-FIVE*. They'll christen me the snipercunt of cocksmith deadbeats, the one men ignore till she rips through their womb of come. So clear off the cobwebs, Faucet-Fist. After your testosterone dries to powdered vanilla Ovaltine, "they" will forget your manhood and remember my mien. *(Leans over and grabs IVAN by the hair)* I said, the name's di Prima, Mister...but *you* can call me *MS. FIFTY-FIVE*. Porn diarist and madam of murderous memoirs.

IVAN
(with his last gasp) Hey....you, lady möte, you...spoke to me... *(slumps forward and stiffens)*

DI PRIMA
(releasing IVAN's head) I always had it in me—or hadn't you noticed? They say the last mute speaks when the loud man dies. (SLOW FADE.)

John Quincy Adams

(1767-1848. His term: 1825-29.)

The sixth President of the United States was the inbred son of the second. John Quincy Adams, scion of John Adams, was the man whose skull typified nineteenth century phrenology's model of the political thinker. A physical refinement of his father, J. Q. boasted a head that appeared slightly too large for his body, a dome made fontanel-frail by generations of incest, a face like a waxwork cooled in a fetal cast.

Though his head resembled a kettle made of salmon-colored aspic, J. Q. wasn't the first Adams to drop face-down from a xenophobe's womb. Washington outsiders had always found the width of an Adams forehead to be faintly grotesque. Nevertheless, the capitol, skull of our nation, swelled with a succession of Adamses like greenbloods gone awry. For nearly a quarter century, appointed aristocrats hid distended temples under diminishing hair, combed whispered curls over brows as bent as Poe's, disguised bulging lobes that shaded the eyes like flaccid oranges. From father's inauguration to end of son's green reign, the nation twisted under the caress of its mutant royalty.

<u>John Quincy was the last politician to emerge from this eugenic Camelot.</u>
Cerebral shiftings and revisions fluttered down to his gene
pool like C notes, augmenting his inheritance of power and
position. His disease made him more than competent for
his office: he reconnoitered the country with an air of regal
dispossession. His very manner convinced the country of
his competence. (This was the kind of perception which
the American public was never again to entertain.)

<u>Private citizens faltered before a man too delicate to steer a plow.</u>
In 1827, when J. Q. visited a dairy farm in Connecticut, he
broke into hives after a particularly humid drift of rain. The
incident was reported reverently in the New England
Gazette; common readers were impressed. He must know
more about meteorology than the Farmer's Almanac, they
surmised.

<u>Fearing dilution, Adams's early republic made concubines of its cousins.</u>
Retreating to a room behind the advisory council chapter,
familiars pressed a special panel webbed in the wall's
arabesque: a brain in bas relief. Presto! the pleasure dome
opened; a canopy flooded with green and purple satin
unfolded; from behind the partition, violin music pervaded
that ornate dungeon where cousins clicked. Kin passed
borders stained with Christian warnings, sank into folds of
familiarity, kissed correspondences and braved unchaste
revelations. Nevertheless, the spot on the wall thought
nothing. No incumbent senator, no newspaper exposé,
railed against corruption in the boudoir.

<u>The congress that kinks together thinks together</u>: volume upon vol-
ume spilled into laity and law. Journalists squinted at
legalese shed by an oligarchy so tight it closed on its own
genitals. *An Adams avoids the corridors of* common *cor-*
ruption, they surmised.

<u>Years later, congenital sickness intervened.</u> Too feeble to stand at
age eighty, John Quincy was confined to a hospital bed.

<u>In the last moments of the last hour of John Quincy's life, he thought</u>:
I am a man of superior yet enfeebling intellect
whose head is rather too large for his body.
My hospital window overlooks a swingset
over which are suspended two knotted strands
of hemp fastened to the grips of knives. After weeks
of treatment and operations, the scene is beginning
to blur. Not that I mourn my view more than my fate.
No wife, no sister, survives. No tears and no loose threads.

To die as I have lived—by an act of incest.
A president's thrust deformed me.
Now viral tongues obliterate my vision.

Fig VII. *Val Demar's Pear*

Val Demar's Pear*

I do not deem it advisable to enter into a description of
the technical details attendant upon the process of pass
ing out of the physical body into the astral body of finer
substance. Any description of this kind, even though it be
merely a suggestion of the facts, might give an untrained
person at least a hint of the process, which might lead
him to experiment and which might bring upon him
undesirable results.

—Swami Panchadasi, *The Astral World*

*As there are seven plagues held in abeyance by
seven angels, seven cosmic elements, and seven
degrees in the Pythagorean scale, so there are
seven rooms in Sorrow's imperial suite. Each room
descends sharply into the next; each successive
room, like each vortex of the etheric body, is suffused with a different hue. The first is violet, the
second, indigo, the third, blue, the fourth, green, the
fifth, yellow, the sixth, orange. The last room is
black, with windows in vivid red.*

*A mist devolves in the corners of a blue-black sky—a sky
the color of a bruise on a prizefighter's arm. Wind screams
at a pitch far too high for howling. The camera pans across
the coast of Marseilles. Backtrack to close-up of the sea: a*

montage of black water, florid sponges, coral turned gray, gasping bass, and anemone fisted like rheumatic hands.
   Cut to a clear sunset falling coral pink on a fortress of institutional buildings. The legend on the gateway to the cobblestone entrance reads De Profundis. As a new voice-over begins, the images dim. The speaker is a late-middle-aged woman with a refined but weighted voice.

I, Alexandra Alline, an invalid with violent motor disturbances, was once the sanguine Professor of Color Therapy at the Piaget Institute in Nice. In the spring of 1961, my colleague, Professor Val Demar and I conducted a series of psycho-sexual experiments in German rooms modeled after those in Poe's "Ligeia" and "Masque of the Red Death." A few of our students had happily volunteered themselves as test subjects, and we expected only the most beneficial effects from our study.

A Chaconne on Catharsis:
The Color Series From "Masque of the Red Death"

First Room	Blue	C1
Second Room	Purple	B1
Third Room	Green	F1
Fourth Room	Orange	D1
Fifth Room	White	(x)
Sixth Room	Violet	B0
Seventh Room	Black and Red	(x) C1

Though our progression of tinted rooms transposed Poe's arrangement exactly, the inner design revealed a cosmology of sources. Each cell enthroned a neurohistorical pastiche, a microcosm starred with literary and sociological chimeras—the pallid, perfumed interiors described by Huysmans, for example, or the imprisoning quarters of Bronte's Jane Eyre—its facets littered with forbidding devices described in the writings of Masoch, De Sade, and Di Bella. On each far wall, miniature false windows were inset with dioramas depicting scenes which the test subjects found particularly disquieting or abrasive: the architecture of Piranesi and Bellmer; Delacroix's paintings of Hell; devices in cast iron—hatchet and cat's paw, brank and bridle—applied to the faces of Bosnian slaves; pornographic lithographs of posed fetuses; and reversible perspective serigraphs of cubist orgies/nameless graves.

Occasionally, and only in certain highly repressed cases, we incorporated the reconstructed childhood sites of the test patient into our design. The brief list of these rare controls is as follows: a fundamentalist grandfather's blasphemous attic; a shadowy farmhouse decorated with almanac calendars, where an embalmed servant stood in his red dinner jacket, obsequiously holding his cap; a hospital death bed; a pedophile's nursery; and a pre-school Jesuit auditorium filled with Spanish saws.

In composition and detail, the rooms owed more to "Ligeia" than to "Masque of the Red Death": the central room of our series was an orange, pentagonal reconstruction of Ligeia's bridal chamber exactly as Poe described it. In this story, as in "The Fall of the House of Usher" and so many others, the architecture is a metaphor for the strictures of the skull; but for our purposes, "Ligeia" seemed Poe's most significant and symptomatic love story.

Descriptions of the rooms proved fiercely various. To some subjects, the "disorderly" and "jarring" rooms felt uncomfortable from the beginning (as indeed, we had meant them to be); to others, the arrangement seemed aesthetically euphonious (with the exception of the quintic, penultimate and ultimate chambers). A certain eccentric subject likened the rooms to a descending line of lights within the body—the colors of the spectrum, which he said were "vorticed" within the spine—that lead from the spiritual to the sensual world. We guessed from this

191

description that his birth had been harrowing and raked with deferred-action trauma.

The test subjects were first put under hypnosis, then told to imagine themselves dying from the effects of a primal realization. With each descent into a lower room, the "doomed" subjects' bodies were tinted by more lurid shades of colored glass. When they reached the last chamber and felt thoroughly resigned to death, the subjects were instructed to commit a last sexual act—the act they most desired and feared—at the point of half-consciousness.

Since the controls of these experiments seemed relatively easy to maintain, no ill effects were anticipated. We believed that it is healthier to explore a subject's sexuality than it is to repress his desire.

Unfortunately, even the healthiest volunteers developed symptoms that earlier psychiatric studies could neither presage nor explain. One man seemed unable to recognize anything for days, then claimed he'd been sitting at the sun's median, with millions of miles of space in all directions. He'd been happy, he explained, before untillions with the heads of cobras locked his skull in a boarhead brank. Another girl smelled burning rubber in the last room; a few seconds later, the ferret cages and tubed matrices of geckos were clogged with amphibious corpses. These unlikely collisions of repression and chance seemed anomalous. We expected no deepening of this interdisciplinary dilemma, but we were wrong.

One subject emerged from the seventh room in a trance-like state, his upturned hands sutured together at the little finger, his palms filigreed with pointillistic lacerations that spelled the nonsense word, *Qliphoth*.[**] Though our bibliothecal expeditions lasted for weeks, Demar and I found no entry for *Qliphoth* in the *Larousse International,* in the *Lexique de la Terminologie Polyptotonique,*[+] in *Webster's Third International Dictionary,* in the Classical Dictionary of de Saumaise, nor in the *Cours de Linguistique Générale* of de Saussure. We attempted to decrypt the word by searching for a coded numerical sequence, pitch-spectrum, or an anagram of a place-name from the subject's childhood, but none seemed even remotely likely. Clearly, the safety of our subject remained obscurely assaulted.

By the Autumn of 1962, we decided to focus our experiment further by adopting a decentralized relationship between subject and psychologist. Our own thoughts were monitored by cranial synapse decoders; transcribed; edited; and finally excised. At length, I myself decided to descend these "vortices" of death and desire—to participate in a fully documented experiment, but without the controls of a clinician's supervision.

The following account is taken from a two-inch TEAC reel of my last half hour prior to losing consciousness and permanently damaging my sense of prioperceptive coherence.

Room Number One: Blue: Voices

My gaze is focused on an infusible perspective. I'm not sure where I am, nor can I find any purpose in recurrences of space and detail. Brightness dims in the length of a dismal hall; ears detect whisper and invocation before eyes can discern the climate of the clinic.

Scenes dissolve, diegetic barriers are obliterated. Running water merges with the sound of a cat waking. Professor Demar is in my office, peering at a doorknob in the shape of a coelacanth. The walls are ringed convexities, like unshielded speakers. Specimens cast from the organs of my brother's corpse are suspended from the cerulean ceiling, distracting me as his final words had promised.[++] From an inverted autopsy table the apparatus swings above me. I duck under a pancreas of violet frosted glass, its vein-

193

relief dusted with heliotrope and hyacinth shavings.

My footsteps echo against the bald surfaces of the room. A woman's face—an indigo rhomboid smear reflected in the mirror's tessellations—changes shape, color and sex, becoming someone other than myself. I name this person "Reynold" and hear him act:

"Do you always wear turquoise gloves?" Reynold asks the jaundiced clinician, as he sets his lead soldier astride an escalator of files.

"Only when I kill. The gloves make me notorious, which gives me the space to work." The room dims.

Reynold chuckles. "Lucky man. You've always loved your work, and now it is loved by others."

Demar presses a toggle switch; speaker horns, which comprise the walls, amplify our speech; and the room itself becomes our sounding board. "Yes, but who am I?" he asks. "To you, I mean."

"My colleague?"

Demar laughs. "You have no colleague in solitary, therefore 'we' are you. But for me, of course, identity is problematic. Which is why I require your expertise: I want you to find the one who stops me from killing people."

Reynold no longer applies blue enamel to my pinkie nail. Inadvertently, I paint my cheek as I bend forward to listen.

Nerves gather at the corners of the ceiling. Nerves gather at the corners of the ceiling. Nerves gather at the corners of the ceiling.

"Why do you think someone's running interference? No corporation is interested in us, nor is the Academy of Science. The government is oblivious and the police have never embraced the cause of pacifism. So your anti-assassin would have to be a person without obligations. Acting out of sync with any known agency."

"That's precisely what I mean." *The room is shrouded in shadow. Now there are only voices.*

"Even so, what's the payoff? Why bother to murder at all

when there are agencies for that sort of thing? The police, for example."

"Because killing is a blast of organ music rising through a heap of porcupines. Your throat clogs with vomit, as if you were fucking the Beast from The Revelations."

Reynold feigns a disinterested yawn. "I wouldn't know."

Demar gurgled his concurrence. "Besides, I'm dead. Which means there's an agency you've overlooked."

Demar pauses before looking at Reynold, his gaze lost in the convolutions of fluted mirror and perigynous chandelier. Reynold ignores him; a tiny ray of sapphire light travels up my forearm, reassuring me his attention is ultimately mine.

"I know you write love poems in my absence," Demar explains. "But it is only my absence which makes you imagine you love me."

Reynold chokes on a clot of self-revulsion. "I'm—I don't understand you...."

Demar hums a tune that disturbs me—

—lingering on the A-Sharp until I howl to drown out his voice. Wall and autopsy merge to a single faucet-spray of royal blue—a luminous trickle in darkness, which gradually brightens to hyaline.

Rob Hardin

Room Number Two: Purple: The Dome

I am splintering but cogent. My fragments whip through slate blue smoke on a breeze like an intensifying fear. Cerulean thins to hints of amethyst:

I meet Professor Demar in a lilac-pale drawing room in Bis Rue, Ordener. On loan from a longstanding patient, the ornate sitting room overlooks the confines of a hillside park; from our vantage, on the ground floor of a landmark building, only the first swerve of the lane is visible. Gamely, Demar points to an ignited wino lying on a bench, his assailant a diminishing blur at the park's far edge. As Demar and I shake hands briskly, a fly dives into my vision, its black husk widening like the hole in a strip of burning film. When my focus returns and I stop gazing fixedly at the floor, he nods faintly. I do not question the concordance of fly and wino, I simply accept it as one of Demar's unsettling signs.

He asks me a lot of questions; I get the job. The girandole on the far wall distracts me from my triumph: every face I can remember, including that of my mother, coalesces briefly among the vortices of its embellishments. Gradually, these faces are superseded by his; by moist violet eyes topped with sweeping alchemical brows—white arches fanged at the vertex—the usual smile underlined by a goatee too barbed for Lucifer Himself.

After this initiation, Demar accompanies me in everything. At dusk, the hyacinthine walls dissolve; floor and ceiling float off in opposite directions; and sudden space enfolds us like a sea of emerald air.

Room Number Three: Green: The Heart

I am changed by the color of stanzas; by the stanza— Italian for room—*which delivers by measured cadenza the impression of space between frames. When Demar suggests the solution to my Descartian split lies in his clinician's embrace, I feign repulsion. But in the lawn by the lane of procedure, I exult in the syntax of grass.*

In an Italian neighborhood in Chambeyron, on Sunday in sliding half-light, I find half-naked old people sitting in a disordered garden. Their shorts and socks, their flaccid bellies, disgust me, as does the ragged blue grass. Cerulean weeds surround their moldering sandals; at their feet, on a hospital cot affixed with an oscilloscope and barium injector, I discover my long-buried stepmother's bed-ridden corpse.

A disheveled hospital orderly peers down at her with mere indifference.

Val Demar is dressed as a Lower Quarter peasant, a film of indigo soot obscuring his complexion.

"Wasn't treating 'er proper," he says.

"Who wasn't what," I reply.

Demar gestures toward the sky. *"The others,"* he whispers.

Overhead, fanning away shreds of cloud, I see a crowd of giant blue suits with *heretic's forks*[+++] for heels and fragments of my upper torso—a strip of muscle, a clump of guts, a tongue—for heads. Their jackets appear to be made of worn rubber, like the off-yellow mat I've often avoided in my grandmother's bathroom. The lapels quiver as the suits wave white linen gloves at the dead woman on the ground.

Room Number Four: Orange: Desire

I stand at the core of a nova that blazes outward from my spleen, radiating a meshwork. I focus my pain into a single, impaling beam and materialize in the center room of the series. Everything I do seems posthumous—alive in the rueful eye of a bride gone blind.

Rob Hardin

IN THE BRIDAL CHAMBER OF "LIGEIA", I find myself spread-eagled on a bridal couch, my limbs slip-knotted to slim coral sarcophagi. I lie in a vast, pentagonal chamber in a high, slight tower with battlements for parapet embrasures. The entire south-eastern facet, dominated by a single, gray window, lends a cadaverous pallor to all phenomena that occur outside the bedroom: moonrise, sunset, and noon seem merely to reflect the world outside my sex. A ceiling patterned with Druidic, Egyptian, Hebrew, Tibetan, and Celtic devices burgeons with the topograph of a suspended, dinner-jacketed corpse; in each corner spans a miniature mural of Shiva, Lord Yama, or Nrimshediva. A tangerine lantern licked with chromatic fire and suspended from a bronze chain hangs from the center of the ceiling. Backless, overstuffed couches extend to the room's center like supernumerary beds, or fingers to the bridal couch's palm—a couch of solid apricot, canopied in cadaver gray to deflect thoughts of death or discorporation; finished with a mixture of peach varnish and pasteurized XYY semen; and speckled with the treated blood of suicidal donors. Invisible walls loom—draped with dense orange curtains that cast kinetic shadows over dangling candelabrum and edge-obscured window, as wind from a concealed vent keeps the draperies tremulous with a rinse of ascending air. The drapes themselves are arabesqued with sutric couplings in patterns of orange and red; dual-imaged congresses that, when seen from a distance, represented formally-dressed couples frozen hand in hand—but from closer vantage, reveal unruly nudes engaged in acts of improvised torture, multiple masturbation, pan-fetishism, AI-random formations of eroticised organs, visceral scarification, the simultaneous sodomy of all orifices (including the eyes and pores), bestiality among the unborn, pathogenic exhibitionism, embryophilia, autopsophilia, tomomania, and other exquisite archetypes of arousal. Such pleasures, glimpsed in mid-flux, appear unbearably vivid. Synthetic wind tracks the asymmetrical walls, investing the room with an agonized and sinuous energy.

Room Number Five: White: Being

I return to an arid reality which seems impermanent because arrived at by a witless leap. The mist, the blue-black sky, the wind, recur. The camera returns to the coast of Marseilles, the sea, and dying sea-life. Voice-over: an African American girl with a South Carolina slur.

Ro-anna

I don't eat no more fishes or any like that. One day there was a chicken runnin' round my grandma's house; next thing, it was on the table. I say, 'Excuse me,' and I never ate no more pig, or no cow—not after I seen that eff'n chicken walk.

Montage of farms, hatcheries, wildlife preserves, tundras and deserts. The animals stare at the camera like the abandoned prisoners of rest homes.

All animals gots a heartbreak, so they all suffer—lobster begs, fish cries, otter looks at you like a holy man. Some may preach they only for food. Me, I just wanna do right by all that's livin'...

The camera returns to lower regions....

Room Number Six: Violet: The Dome

This room is dim, like the purple blood of plums.
Demar's head, crown pressed in a skull-splitter, jaw tortured by an oral pear, explodes; the skull flies apart in curvicular segments; blood reigns.

199

As he passes through the color ring at the center of the purple dome, Demar glimmers with fluctuant iridescences in the shadows and crevices of his body. Wrinkles ripple gold and silver, until his body seems a rainbow with metallic highlights:

With every shift of the skull, his crown flashes violet. His forehead pulses indigo; a glowing blue tendril extends from the pituitary gland through his head and caresses the window's hyacinthine glow. His throat beams blue; his green chest opens on a wound of leaves surrounding a vibrant emerald. The yellow hue of his solar plexus intensifies with each cry of pain or laughter. His orange genitals drool teardrops of pearl-white phosphorous; the base of his spine reddens angrily as he approaches the hole. Less distinctly, muddier lights glimmer in the lower part of his pelvis; between his knees; and in his ankles.

He pulls my head down to his groin, his orange penis flickering with each bloodlit pulse. He sighs as I suck him, but I can feel no glans-tip touch my throat. (What if his organ's nervure lay in its light alone, and thrilled as its radiance grazed the inside of my mouth?) Groaning, he pushes me between his knees, where I kiss him with unqualified abjection. When I reach his dun-colored ankles, the pear and head-crusher fastened to his skull tighten: bone and brain fly apart in ovaline segments, like the spurting petals of a violet engorged with blood.

Room Number Seven: Black & Red: Nonbeing, Retrogression

THE LAST PORTAL BRINGS ME TO THE POLLUTED SPHERE OF CENOTAPHS—A SPHERE THAT SLOWLY DARKENS INTO THE PRESENT WORLD. ITS GLOOM AFFLICTS ME WITH A PSYCHOSOMATIC ILLNESS THAT PROVES INCURABLE AND RAPIDLY DETERIORATES INTO A TUMOR AT THE BASE OF THE SPINE. UNINTEN-

TIONALLY, I HAVE LINKED THE TEMPORAL WORLD TO THE TENTH SPHERE OF THE ELEVENTH SEPHROTH, QLIPHOTH: LILITH.

The red door stands at the right border of the waking world, in a wasteland of ice and wind. It seals off the entrance to a desolate domain. I open it by pulling on the stems of a brace which is itself a cryptogram:

The door flies open. Catapulted by my curiosity, fluids rush past like liquid missiles, a siege of javelins gripped by mysterious winds. Bile and spinal slime whip through the air, spattering the ice with purged brown excrescence and pus-marbled blood.

Shift shift. There is no transition. I stand in the hallway of an Appalachian tenement, opening an apartment door on a train of ill-lit rooms.

The place seems subterranean, like a basement. Descending emotionally, I enter, heel touching level floor. I turn to face what I assume will be unrelieved squalor.

The wood floor is shiny with carmine paint. A few feet past the door, there is a clutter of surgical knives and shredded pajamas. The deeper I look, the darker the apartment's disorder.

Like highchair feeders pulled down by an impulsive child, silver aluminum trays lie scattered through the first few rooms. Each tray brims with a whitish, pallid solution. Submerged in it are the leg-stumps of naked lost children: three-year-old boys snatched out of life. They gaze and sway, reaching for my hand as I walk, fascinated eyes unaware of their own slow deliquescence. At the edges of their amputations, the skin is layered like cabbage. The outer layers have become so water-logged that they are nearly transparent; the inner layers are white and devoid of blood.

"Making pee," one of them sings as I pass.

It is the most tragic and disgusting thing I have ever seen. *Who did this,* I think. *How could anyone mutilate a living child?*

I enter the next room. More trays—but there is also spillage on the red floor. In the corner, a piss-vampire with the feminized face of Demar, curls next to one of the trays—white, clammy, hairless except for a thin widow's peak, her skeletal ribs and worm-viscous teats exposed, jeans pulled down past withered buttocks. She sucks the urine from a child's penis and gapes at me with wide, sallow eyes—dreaming, like the children, but haunted, emotionless. A cave-parasite with the cast of Albert Fish.

Later, I talk to the ghoul with Demar's angular face. I learn I've entered one of the lower realms—places where souls who have devolved for lifetimes enter the final stages of non-being. The cenobites of Freemasons, the creatures of the hellish planets in Hinduism—all reside there, in regions which the suicide reaches by forbidden doors, or the troubled soul visits in dreams.

END OF TAPE

Flashes of paralytic seizures, barbiturate IV's, shock treatments, lobotomy knives. Cut to the sea: A cloudbank burns in the center of a crimson sky—a sky the texture of the ruptured spleens of bees. The camera pans across the blackening shoreline: on the ledge of the beach is a complex of mirrored buildings.

Some time remained before intravenous rushes of synthetic adrenaline could hurl me back into life. Dully, I dreamed of Hans Bellmer's ageless face; once aware, I awoke among pedophiles in a death ward in Marseilles, where I learned my tape had served as evidence in the Court which condemned my colleague for our studies. The ward seemed an auditorium filled with Spanish saws; for me, there seemed no prayer of prison or execution. I could not move; I could not raise my voided voice to a whisper, let alone manage more than a mental shriek.

Through the crisis of Qliphoth, my fragmented selves rejoin.

Presently, I convulse alone in a hospital bed, survived by neither Demar nor any other subject of my studies. My psyche feels desecrated and devolved, my features seem a reptilian shorthand for thwarted greed. Hourly, I repulse my orderlies with the same lizard smile. Unable to change my signal motivations, I can only fail to conceal their slight, bacillic stirrings.

At the institute, I thought I'd reached a plane of intellectual understanding: my visualizations appeared so intense, so magnified by that chain of colored rooms, that all knowledge seemed humane and necessary. But these images were merely the child-corpses of Lilith; naively, I entered that matrix of murderous spheres. The lower Sephiroth teems with creatures willing to trample the faces of fledglings in a bum-rush of ruthless ascendancy: they trade in impossible promises of destiny and redemption. Not recognizing such demons, I dealt with Samael, the demigod of science; now I wait in the grimmest game-room of Lilith for the chance to die and ascend to what I've been.

Now that I've suffered the process, I require the skeleton's key: I've watched addicts and novices descend to monastic orders of hellhounds who scratch and whine at

Rob Hardin

Dachau's doors; I've studied the shame-pained faces of the self-betrayed. I know that nothing but eons of perseverance can lift me to the realms above this abyss; to the kiss of the Crowd of Gods; to ascend past the lower realms to my last release; past the final rooms of my closing fists—those masks in gridded black with sanguine slits.

Fig VII. *Val Demar's Pear*

The End

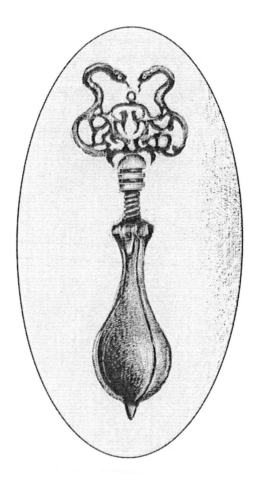

Rob Hardin is a writer and studio musician who lives in a once-lethal sector of the Lower East Side. His writing has been praised in *Downtown Magazine, Locus,* and *Poets & Writers;* and quoted in *Keyboard, Mondo 2000,* and *Terminal Velocity.* As a keyboardist and vocalist, he has played with Nation of Abel, Saqquari Dogs, Pillbox, Pitch Black, PiL, 22 Brides, and members of the Psychedelic Furs. His recent album projects include Speedway, Truth, and Cherry Red. Currently working on a second novel that he describes as *Bellmer noir,* he avows that art can, in the abstract, vindicate loved ones who were cheated out of life, and confesses that writing is his way of getting dissonant counterpoint—the chamber music of nightmares and empty attics—out of his system.

Printed in the United States
1266500001B/226-252